ASTRID LINDGREN

Mardie

Illustrated by Ilon Wikland

Translated by Patricia Crampton

D0063002

A Magnet Book

Also by Astrid Lindgren in Magnet books

Lotta
Karlson on the Roof
Karlson Flies Again

This edition first published in Great Britain 1979
by Methuen Children's Books Ltd
Originally published in Sweden as Madicken
by Rabén & Sjögren Bokförlag, Sweden
Published in Great Britain as Madicken *1963*
by Oxford University Press
Magnet edition published 1979
by Methuen Children's Books Ltd
11 New Fetter Lane, London EC4P 4EE

Copyright © 1960 Astrid Lindgren
This English translation copyright © 1979
Methuen Children's Books Ltd
Illustrations copyright © 1960 Ilon Wiklana

Printed in Great Britain by
Richard Clay (The Chaucer Press) Ltd
Bungay, Suffolk

ISBN 0 416 87610 2

Contents

I

A Summer day in Junedale

Mardie lived outside a small Swedish town in a big, red house, down by a stream. Mama and Papa and little sister Elizabeth and a black poodle called Sasso and a kitten called Goodie lived there too. And so did Alma. Mardie and Elizabeth lived in the nursery, Alma lived in the maid's room, Sasso in a basket in the hall and Goodie in front of the kitchen stove. Mama lived almost all over the house and so did Papa, except when he was down at the newspaper office writing, so that people in the town had something to read.

Mardie's real name was Margaret, but when she was little she called herself Mardie. And now that she was big, almost seven, she was still called Mardie. It was only when she had been up to something and had to be spoken to sternly that she was called Margaret. She was called Margaret often. Elizabeth was called Lisbet and seldom had to be spoken to sternly, but Mardie had so many mad ideas and never stopped to think . . . until afterwards. Then she was sorry. She was so willing to be good and obedient, that it was a pity she didn't always succeed.

'That child gets ideas as fast as a pig blinks,' said
Ida, and that was true.

Ida came on Fridays to wash and scrub.

It was Friday today and Mardie was sitting on the
edge of the jetty, watching Ida doing the washing.
Mardie was happy, her pinafore pocket was full of
sweet, golden plums which she ate from time to time,
splashing her bare feet in the water and singing for
Ida's benefit:

> '*ABCD*,
> *The cat is on the spree.*
> *The cat is on the spree, my dove,*

2

for nothing else but love.
KLMN,
She said then.
She said then, my dove,
For nothing else but love.'

Mardie had almost made up the rhyme by herself. A bit of it came from Mama's old ABC book and a bit from a song which Alma sang when she was washing up. Mardie thought it was a good song to sing when you were washing clothes and eating plums, but Ida didn't agree.

'Dearie me, what a row,' she said. 'Don't you know any pretty songs?'

'I think that *is* a pretty song,' said Mardie. 'But the ones you sing are prettier. Please, Ida, sing that one about Jesus the railway to the sky.'

But Ida wouldn't sing while she was washing and that was just as well, because although Mardie liked to hear the song about Jesus railway, it always made her cry. She had only to think of it to become quiet, her eyes shiny with tears. It was such a sad song, about a little girl who thinks she can take the train all the way to Heaven and meet her mother, who is dead . . . No, Mardie didn't dare to think about it just then. All Ida's songs were equally sad. The mothers did nothing but die, and the fathers were always down at the pub drinking, until the children died too. Then the fathers went home and cried and were dreadfully sorry and promised never to drink again . . . but it was too late!

Mardie sighed as she took a fresh plum. How glad she was that her own mother was alive and in the red house! Every night when Mardie was in bed and had said *Our Father*, she prayed an extra prayer that she

3

and Lisbet and Mama and Papa and Alma and Ida and Abe Nilsson should be allowed to go to Heaven all at the same time. Of course, it would be best if they didn't have to go at all, Mardie thought, because they were having such a good time here. But she didn't dare ask God for that, because it might upset Him.

Ida liked people to cry at her songs.

'Now you know, Mardie,' said Ida, 'now you know what a bad time poor children have. So you can be grateful, because you're as lucky as a jewel set in gold.'

Of course, Mardie *was* as lucky as a jewel set in gold. She had Mama and Papa and Lisbet and Alma and Ida and Abe Nilsson and she lived in Junedale. You couldn't live in a better place. If anyone had asked Mardie how it looked this is what she might have said:

'Oh, it's an ordinary red house! It's like a *house*, of course. The nicest place is the kitchen; Lisbet and I play in the log box and we help Alma with the baking. No, actually the nicest place is the attic; Lisbet and I play hide-and-seek there and sometimes we dress up as cannibals and pretend to eat people. We have fun on the verandah, too. We climb in and out of the windows and pretend to be pirates climbing up and down the ropes of our ship. There are lots of birch trees all round the house and I climb them, but Lisbet doesn't because she's too small, only five. Sometimes I climb on the woodshed roof too. The woodshed and the workshop and the mangle shed and the wash-house are all in a red building right up against the Nilssons' fence. If you sit on the woodshed roof you can look straight into the Nilssons' kitchen, and that's fun. And it's fun turning the mangle when Alma and Ida are in the mangle shed, mangling. But in any case, the stream is the best place of all. We are allowed on the washing jetty because the water isn't deep there, but further out it is deep. The road is on the other side. We've got a currant hedge there so no one can see what we're doing. But we can hide behind the hedge and hear what people are saying as they go past, isn't that marvellous?'

That's more or less what Mardie would say, if you asked her what Junedale is like.

And she really did hide behind the hedge and hear what people were saying as they went past. Sometimes she heard them say:

'Oh look, what a pretty little girl!'

Then Mardie knew they must have caught sight of Lisbet, standing tiptoe on the gate and smiling all over her face. Mardie didn't think she herself was a pretty little girl at all, but she was very pleased when people said Lisbet was. Everyone thought Lisbet pretty, even Ida.

'I tell you, I tell you, she's as pretty as a picture,' said Ida.

'And good, too,' said Mardie, biting Lisbet in the arm, just a little bit. That made Lisbet laugh, as if Mardie had tickled her. Almost all of Lisbet was soft and smooth and pretty, but she had little white teeth and she bit Mardie in the cheek as hard as she could.

'Oh, you're as sweet as a pickle,' she said, laughing still more.

There was nothing soft and smooth and sweet about Mardie, but she had a nice sunburned little face, a pair of bright blue eyes and thick brown hair. And she was as straight and slim and nimble as a cat.

'She was never meant to be a girl,' said Ida. 'I tell

5

you, I tell you, she ought to have been a boy, as sure as
I was born.'

Mardie herself was quite happy to look the way she
did.

'I'm like my Papa,' she said, 'and that's marvellous.
It means I'm sure to get married.'

Lisbet was a little worried – what if *she* were not to
get married? But she was like Mama, everyone said so.
Not that she was particularly worried about getting
married, but if Mardie was, Lisbet was too. She wanted
to do *exactly* the same as Mardie.

'You're too small to think about such things,' said
Mardie, patting Lisbet on the head. 'Wait till you're
big and have started school like me.'

It was not quite true that Mardie had started school, but they had her name down and in a week's time she would be going. So she was almost a schoolgirl.

'In any case, perhaps I shan't get married after all,' said Mardie, in order to comfort Lisbet. In her heart of hearts she could not quite understand what was so clever about getting married. But if it had to be, it would be to Abe Nilsson, Mardie had decided, though Abe didn't know yet.

Ida had finished her washing and Mardie had eaten all her plums. Then Lisbet came trotting down to the jetty. She had been playing on the verandah with Goodie, but she was tired of that now and wanted to know what Mardie was doing.

'Mardie,' said Lisbet, 'what shall we do?'

> *Take a couple of cats and go driving,*
> *driving across the snow*
> *and use their tails for reins,'*

said Mardie. That was the right answer, that was what Abe always said.

'Ha ha, I've done that already,' said Lisbet, 'with Goodie . . . and used his tail for reins . . . on the verandah!'

'Then I shall scratch you,' said Mardie. 'If you've been pulling Goodie's tail I'm going to scratch you too, so now you know.'

'I haven't at all,' said Lisbet. 'I didn't pull it a little bit. I just held on to his tail, it was Goodie who pulled and tugged so dreadfully.'

Even Ida looked sternly at Lisbet.

'Don't you know, Lisbet, that God's angels weep till it pours when children are unkind to animals?'

'Ha ha, but then it rains,' said Lisbet. 'And it's *not*

7

raining now.'

No, it wasn't raining now. The sun was shining warmly and the sweetest scent came from the sweet-peas in the round bed, the bees were humming over the grass and the stream ran calmly and silently past Junedale. You could feel all over your body that it was summer, Mardie thought, splashing her feet in the warm water.

'I tell you, I tell you, all this heat is unnatural,' said Ida, wiping the sweat from her forehead. 'It's like washing clothes in the Nile in Africa, not like being at home in Sweden.'

That was all Ida said, but it was all Mardie needed. After all, her ideas came as fast as a pig blinks.

'I know what we'll do, Lisbet,' said Mardie. 'We'll play Moses in the bulrushes!'

Lisbet bounced up and down with excitement.

'Can I be Moses?'

Ida laughed.

'Ho ho, you'd make a lovely Moses!'

But then Ida had to go and hang up her washing and Mardie and Lisbet were left alone on the banks of the Nile.

In the evening, when the light was out in the nursery and everything was quiet, Mardie used to tell stories to Lisbet. Sometimes she told stories about 'ghosts and murderers and wars', although that meant that Lisbet had to come into Mardie's bed, otherwise she didn't dare to listen. But sometimes Mardie told stories from the Bible, the ones she had heard from Ida. So Lisbet knew quite well who Moses was. She knew that he had been put in a basket in the water and Pharaoh's daughter, who was a princess in the land of

Egypt, came down and found him there. Moses in the bulrushes, that was a good game! There was an empty washtub on the bank of the stream which would do well for Moses . . . Lisbet climbed in right away.

'No,' said Mardie. 'It can't stay on land, Moses wouldn't be in the bulrushes. Get out of the basket, Lisbet!'

Lisbet obeyed and Mardie pushed the tub out into the water. It was heavy, but Mardie was strong. There weren't many bulrushes in the stream, but right outside the wash-house door there was a big clump of them. If it had not been there you would have been able to see from the Junedale jetty right over to Abe

Nilsson's jetty, but you couldn't now. Mardie thought it was a pity, but Mama thought it was a good thing. Mama definitely thought the less they saw of the Nilssons the better, but why, was more than anyone could understand. After all, you were given eyes so that you could see as much as possible. Just now, it was a good thing that the clump *was* there, otherwise Moses would have had no bulrushes to lie in.

It was hard work getting the tub there. Mardie and Lisbet tugged until they were red in the face, but at last it was right in among the bulrushes. Lisbet climbed into the tub and got comfortable, but then she fell silent and began to look worried.

'Mardie, do you know what?' she said. 'The water's coming in to my drawers.'

'Oh, it'll dry in a moment,' said Mardie. 'It'll dry after I've saved you.'

'Save me soon,' said Lisbet, and Mardie promised. In fact she could have begun at once, but she looked down at her striped cotton pinafore – Pharaoh's daughter couldn't possibly be dressed like that, it wouldn't look right.

'Wait a moment, Lisbet,' said Mardie, 'I'll be back soon. I'm just going to go and see Mama.'

But Mama was not in. She had gone to the market, and Alma was down in the cellar. Mardie had to get hold of some princess's clothes as best she could. She looked around for something that would do. In a corner of the bedroom she found Mama's négligé, which was made of light blue silk. Mardie tried it on; oh, it was wonderful! Perhaps the real Pharaoh's daughter had one just like it when she went down to the river that day, long ago. Perhaps she had a veil

11

over her hair too . . . Mardie rummaged in the linen cupboard and found a thin white kitchen curtain, which she put over her hair. Then she looked at herself in the bedroom looking-glass. She was so beautiful that it made her shiver. Pharaoh's daughter must have looked just like that.

Lisbet had been enjoying herself meanwhile, even though she was quite wet in her tub. The rushes waved to and fro in the wind, dragonflies flew among the stems and tiny, tiny fish were swimming in the water round her. Lisbet watched them over the edge of the tub.

Just then Mardie came striding through the water with Mama's dressing-gown hitched up over her arm. Lisbet thought she looked exactly like Pharaoh's daughter too and laughed with pleasure. Now the game could begin.

'So here you are, little Moses!' said Mardie.

'Yes, I am,' said Lisbet. 'Can I be your little boy?'

'You certainly can,' said Mardie. 'But first of all I've got to save you from this tub. Who put you here?'

'I did it myself,' said Lisbet, but Mardie gave her a very stern look and whispered:

'"My mother did, so that Pharaoh wouldn't kill me".'

Lisbet repeated the words obediently.

'Aren't you glad, little Moses, that you can come to me, since I'm such a grand person?'

'Yes, I am,' Lisbet assured her.

'You shall be grand too,' said Mardie, 'and you shall have new clothes.'

'And dry drawers,' said Lisbet. 'Mardie, do you know what? I think there's a hole in the tub.'

12

'Quiet,' said Mardie. 'The crocodiles will be coming soon, and they eat children. I think I had better save you right away.'

'Defuntly,' said Lisbet.

But it's difficult saving children from the Nile, as Mardie soon realized. Lisbet hung round her neck like a great lump and the négligé kept on trailing in the water.

'There's an awful lot of crocodiles here,' panted Mardie, wobbling towards the bank. 'I think I'll take you to the Nilssons' jetty instead, it's closer.'

'There's Abe,' said Lisbet.

Mardie stopped dead.

'Is he?' she said. 'Get down, Lisbet, you can walk on your own!'

But Lisbet wouldn't.

'I can't do that if I'm being Moses.'

And she wrapped her arms round Mardie's neck as tight as she could.

'I daren't, because of the crocertiles,' she explained.

'There aren't any crocodiles here,' said Mardie. 'We're not playing any more. Get down, do!'

But still Lisbet wouldn't, and Mardie got angry. Lisbet's arms were holding her very tightly round the neck, but it would be easy for Mardie to pull them off, if only she didn't have Mama's négligé to think of. It kept on trailing in the water and she had to hold on to it with both hands. So all she could do was to shake herself crossly to try and get rid of Lisbet. And Abe was standing on the Nilssons' jetty, enjoying the fun.

'Don't shake her off into the Abyss,' he said, spitting into the water.

Mardie knew quite well that there was a deep hole

called the Abyss in one spot near the Nilssons' jetty,
but just then she was so angry she could only think
of making Lisbet get down. So she shook and hit out
backwards like a wild thing, without looking where
she was going.

'I daren't, because of the crocertiles,' squeaked
Lisbet again. That was all, and then there was a
splash. Mardie and Lisbet had disappeared into the
Abyss.

They might have stayed there, there might have
been no more little girls in Junedale, if Abe had not
been standing where he was.

But he calmly picked up the boat-hook lying on the

jetty and cast it out towards the Abyss. And he made a catch. When he pulled it in again, two wet little girls were hanging on to the boat-hook. They scrambled on to the landing-stage, Lisbet howling like a banshee.

'Be quiet!' said Mardie. 'Be quiet, Lisbet, otherwise we'll never be allowed down by the stream again.'

'Why did you have to jump into the Abyss with me, then?' howled Lisbet. She didn't intend to stop crying all that quickly, she'd only just begun. She glared at Mardie.

'I'll tell Mama!'

'You mustn't do that,' said Abe.

'Tell-tale-tit, your tongue shall be slit,' said Mardie. But then she remembered that this soaking, clinging thing she had on was Mama's négligé and that would tell tales even if Lisbet didn't.

'Come on and I'll give you each a sugar bun,' said Abe.

What was so wonderful about Abe was not only that he was fifteen years old and could pull people out of the stream with a boat-hook, but he could bake sugar buns as well and sell them in the market-place. His father should really have baked them and his mother should have sold them in the market, but Abe usually had to do everything. Mardie felt sorry for him. Abe wanted to be a sailor and sail the seas through raging storms, he didn't want to bake at all. But he had to, since his father didn't want to either. When Ida sang her sorrowful songs about poor children whose 'father was drinking his gin', Mardie sometimes imagined to herself that they were about Mr Nilsson, although it was only on Saturdays that Mr Nilsson drank his gin. All the same, Abe had to bake sugar buns all week

15

instead of being at sea sailing through storms, poor Abe!

But when you've been into the Abyss sugar buns are exactly what you need. Lisbet quietened down. She chewed her bun and stared gloomily at her wet clothes.

'Mardie, you said I would be dry after you'd saved me . . . I don't think!'

But when Mama came home a little later she found her two little girls quite dry and dressed again, in the kitchen with Alma. They had put Sasso in the wood basket and were pretending that he was a circus lion. Mardie was showing off his tricks to Alma and Lisbet. It cost two pence to see the circus lion, but not real money, only trouser buttons.

'Because it isn't a real lion either,' said Lisbet, 'so trouser buttons are all right.'

Out on the clothes-line, between the apple trees hung not only Ida's pillow cases and handkerchiefs, but two little dresses and a blue négligé.

Mama kissed Mardie, then she kissed Lisbet, and then she began to take out what she had in her basket.

'I think we'll make soup for lunch,' she told Alma, taking out carrots and cauliflower and leeks and putting them on the kitchen table. 'And then we'll have pancakes.'

Then she turned back to her little girls.

'What have you been doing all day?'

There was absolute silence in the kitchen. Lisbet gave Mardie a scared look and Mardie, her eyes down cast, stared at her big toe as if she had never seen it before.

'Well, what *have* you been doing?' asked Mama again.

16

'We've been washing and rinsing out our clothes,' said Mardie unwillingly. 'And your négligé too . . . that was good ,wasn't it ?'

'*Margaret*,' said Mama.

Out on the clothes-line the washing fluttered gently in the summer breeze and over at the Nilssons' joyful notes could be heard:

'*Oh it's great to be rocked on the ocean blue*
As free as a bird in the sky . . .'

It was Abe, singing as he baked the sugar buns.

2

Richard

Mardie had started school and it was great fun. It was fun to have an ABC book in a fine green cover with a label on it saying Margaret, Class I. Margaret not Mardie, because a schoolgirl can't be called Mardie. It was fun to have a slate and a sponge tied to it by a string and an old hair-oil bottle full of water which you splashed on the slate when you wanted to clean it. It was fun to have slate pencils and a pencil box to put them in and a school satchel made of canvas to put the pencil box in. And best of all . . . in the ABC book there was a cock! The cock laid farthings till they clattered, if you were a good schoolgirl and did your lessons.

Yes, it really was fun to start school and on the first day Mardie was already sighing and saying:

'Oh, why do we have to have a Christmas holiday!'

Of course that was nearly four months away, but still!

Mardie showed the ABC book and the slate and pencil box to Lisbet and Mama and Papa and Ida and Alma and Abe Nilsson. She allowed Lisbet to turn over the pages of the ABC book and write something on the slate, but with lots of stern warnings. Every

morning when Mardie went to school, Lisbet stayed in the living-room, wishing she was the one who was walking off with that fine school bag on her back. It was such a long time before Mardie came home again, Lisbet thought. And when she did come, she had homework. She sat in the nursery working so that you could hear her all over the house.

'ABC,' she read. 'ABC!'

Lisbet could not understand why you had to go on repeating ABC for such a long time, but then she wasn't a schoolgirl.

Every day Papa asked at lunchtime:

'Well, Mardie, how did you get on at school?'

'Marvellous,' said Mardie. 'I'm the best in the class.'

'Who says so?' said Mama. 'You or the teacher?'

'We both say so,' said Mardie.

Mama and Papa looked at each other happily. There now! They had been worrying quite unnecessarily; school can turn even tomboys like Mardie into

19

human beings.

But the days passed and Mardie was no longer quite so eager to do her homework. Mama had to remind her to do her sums and there was not much more ABC to be heard from the nursery. All you could hear was the usual noise of Mardie and Lisbet climbing on the furniture and overturning the nursery chairs. One day you could hear something else as well: Mardie singing.

'*Come, Adolfina, come, Adolfina, kiss me quick,*' she sang. Mama did not like that.

'Really Margaret,' she said, 'what a silly rubbishy song, who taught you that?'

Mama just didn't know! She didn't know what they had at the Nilssons'. Something marvellous . . . a gramophone! A strange-looking thing with a big, big trumpet on it. Mr Nilsson played '*Come, Adolfina*,' on the gramophone every day and danced with Mrs Nilsson. It squeaked and scratched and squawked a lot but you could still hear '*Adolfina*' coming out of the trumpet.

Now the fact was, that Mama seemed to have something against the Nilssons. She really didn't like Mardie to go there, though no-one could imagine why.

'Now Mardie,' repeated Mama, 'who taught you that silly thing?'

Mardie turned red.

'It was . . . it was Richard,' she said. She didn't want to say that she had learned it at the Nilssons.

'Who is Richard?' asked Lisbet.

'Richard . . . is in my class,' said Mardie hastily.

'I see,' said Mama. 'I don't believe you should be seeing too much of that boy.'

A few days later the cock in the ABC book had laid a farthing for Mardie, although she really hadn't been reading very well recently. For a farthing you could get a lollipop in the little shop beside the school. Mardie promised Lisbet a lollipop and Lisbet was waiting all day. At last Mardie came home from school and Lisbet ran down to the sitting-room to meet her.

'Oh, Lisbet,' said Mardie, 'Richard ate your lollipop.'

'Richard should have a spanking,' said Lisbet, very upset.

Yes, Richard certainly needed a good telling-off. That was not the last time he did something wrong.

One day Mardie came home with only one of her galoshes. The other was lost. And it had been such a fine one, black and shiny, with a red lining.

'Where's your other galosh?' asked Mama.

'Richard took it and threw it in the canal,' said Mardie.

'Richard should have a spanking,' said Lisbett.

Mama got very annoyed with this Richard.

'It really is most unfortunate that you should have a boy like that in your class,' she said. 'I think I shall have to go and talk to your teacher.'

But Mama had so much to do that she had no time to go and see the teacher and Richard went on with his silly tricks. He thought up something new almost every day.

Mardie came home with a big ink stain on her new cotton dress . . . Richard, of course! Mardie's slate was cracked in two one day . . . because Richard had thrown it at the wall. He wanted to see if it was a strong slate. It wasn't. Not as strong as all that.

In Mardie's book there was a picture of a queen who had lived in Sweden in the old days. She was dead now but her picture was in the book. One day the queen had a beard and moustaches.

'Really Margaret, why have you been scribbling in your book?' said Mama sternly.

'I didn't do that,' said Mardie. 'Richard did it.'

'Richard should have a spanking,' said Lisbet.

Every day at lunch, Mardie told them all about the awful Richard and his tricks. You simply wouldn't believe how much trouble people had with him. He made a noise during lessons and had to stand in the corner almost all the time.

'And you know what?' said Mardie. 'Today he ate my rubber.'

22

'Ate your rubber?' said Mama, horrified.

'There must be something wrong with that boy,' said Papa.

'Richard should have a spanking,' said Lisbet.

One day Mardie came home from school with a completely new hair style. Richard had been at it again. He'd borrowed Mardie's craft scissors on the way home and snipped off her fringe. And what a fringe it was now!

But Mama's patience was at an end. Things could not be allowed to go on like this for another day.

'I'm going to go and talk to your teacher at school tomorrow,' she said firmly.

'Richard should have . . .' began Lisbet.

'Oh, do be quiet,' cried Mardie angrily. 'Richard can't be spanked. He left school today.'

'Did he?' asked Mama, surprised.

'Yes, he . . . he didn't want to go to school any more,' said Mardie.

'Didn't want to!' said Mama. 'What nonsense. He must be moving and starting at a different school, that's all it is.'

'Yes, perhaps he's going to another school to eat rubbers,' said Lisbet happily.

A day or two later it was Aunt Lottie's birthday. Aunt Lottie lived in the little yellow house right beside the school. Mama took both her girls along to wish her a happy birthday.

Right outside Aunt Lottie's they met the teacher. Mama stopped, no matter how much Mardie pulled at her skirt. Mardie didn't want to talk to the teacher at all, but Mama did.

'How's little Margaret getting on at school?' said Mama. Actually she didn't need to ask, for Mardie herself had said that everything was fine. But Mama thought it would be very nice if the teacher actually said that Mardie was the best in the class.

Strangely enough, the teacher didn't say that.

'Oh well, I expect things will be better when Margaret is a little more used to it,' was what the teacher said. 'A lot of children have difficulty in getting used to school.'

Mama looked thoughtful . . . did the teacher really mean that Mardie was that kind of child? Then what must she think of Richard!

'Yes indeed, and what about that Richard?' said Mama. 'It's a good thing he's left now. It must be a relief to be rid of such a little nuisance.'

'Richard?' said the teacher, surprised. 'We've

24

never had a boy called Richard.'

'Oh, but . . .' Mama began. Then she closed her
mouth and looked sternly at Mardie.

'Richard should have a spanking,' said Lisbet.

Mardie's face was red and she was staring down at
her shoes. A spanking Lisbet said! Somebody was
certainly going to have a spanking, but who? Oh, how
she missed Richard, now he had gone!

3
Mardie and Lisbet have an outing at home

Mardie never talked about Richard any more and Lisbet was sorry about that. She could not understand that Richard no longer existed. She missed him, especially at lunchtimes and sometimes Lisbet would say:

'I wonder what Richard's doing in his new school?'

Then Mardie glared angrily at her, Mama pretended not to have heard, but Papa would laugh and tease Mardie a little.

'Ah yes, Miss Marvellous, you certainly have an imagination! Tell us a bit about how you've been getting on at school . . . without Richard.'

And Mardie told them. Teacher had such a beautiful little gold watch on a long chain and Mia had lots of nits in her hair and the boys fought in the school yard every day and it was great fun sitting in the corridor in the first break eating your sandwiches.

'What do the children have in their sandwiches?' asked Lisbet, who wanted to know everything about the school.

'Sausage and cheese,' said Mardie.

Lisbet sighed. Just think of there being children as

lucky as that! They were allowed to sit in the passage eating sausage and cheese sandwiches and they could have pencil boxes and slates and school satchels, oh, how Lisbet fretted because she could not go to school as well.

Papa went on with his questions. Next day at lunch he asked again:

'Well, Miss Marvellous, how was it at school today?'

Mardie thought. Now that there was no more Richard there wasn't as much to tell, either. But she could always think of something.

'Mia has so many nits, they crawl on the benches,' said Mardie. 'I wish I had some too.'

'Well, thank you very much,' said Mama.

Lisbet was just going to pop in a spoonful of mashed potato, but she put down her spoon.

'At my school,' she said triumphantly, 'at my school all the children have nits in their hair.'

'Schhh,' said Mardie, 'you don't go to school.'

'Oh yes, I do,' said Lisbet, looking stubborn. 'Why should Mardie be the only one to have funny things to talk about?'

Papa laughed.

'So you have a school too, do you? I expect it's the school Richard has moved to.'

Lisbet brightened up, what a marvellous idea! Now she need not only inherit Mardie's clothes and shoes, she could inherit Richard too and have him at her school. Lisbet smiled broadly and nodded.

'Yes, Richard has come to my school and he's got an awful lot of nits in his hair,' she said.

'You're so childish, Lisbet,' said Mardie.

The weeks passed. One Saturday in September

27

Mardie came home from school quite wild with excitement, her eyes shining.

'Is Mama home?' she called as usual, before she was through the door, and then it all came pouring out.

'Mama, we're going to have an outing . . . on Wednesday . . . the whole school. First we're going by train and then we have to walk a long way and then we're going to go up a mountain and sit there eating sandwiches and looking at the view, oh I'm so happy!'

She couldn't stand still; she hopped up and down with joy and flung her arms round Mama, beaming all over her face. But Lisbet stood beside her, gloomy as a thunder cloud. She was silent for a while and then she said solemnly:

'My school's going to have an outing too and we're

going to go on the train and we're going to go up a much higher mountain.'

'You're not at all,' said Mardie.

'Stupid thing!' shouted Lisbet. Then she threw herself head first into Mama's lap, shaking with heart-broken sobs.

'I want to have an outing too and sit on a mountain eating sandwiches!'

Mardie felt sorry for Lisbet.

'You and me can have an outing on our own,' she said.

Lisbet went on crying a little bit to make sure, then she looked up with tear-filled eyes.

'And sit on a mountain?' she asked.

'Perhaps,' said Mardie. 'If we can find one.'

'That's very nice of you, Mardie,' said Mama. 'You two have an outing, that will be fun, won't it Lisbet?'

Mama thought this would be just the day for it, for she and Papa had been invited to the Berglunds for lunch.

'We can pack up a basket and you can take it with you to some nice place,' said Mama, patting Lisbet on the cheek.

'Some nice mountain,' Lisbet corrected her.

Mama got out the red basket which stood on a shelf in the cloakroom and filled it with lots of good things; little meatballs, chipolata sausages, a couple of hard-boiled eggs, a slice of apple tart, a bottle of milk and two buns.

'I'm sure Mama and Papa won't get such a nice lunch at the Berglunds,' said Mardie.

But Mama was in a hurry. She put on her hat and coat, giving Mardie instructions as she did so.

'Don't go too far away, and tell Alma where you're going.'

And to Alma she said:

'Would you please keep an eye on the children, Alma, while I'm out?'

'Yes Madam, I certainly will,' said Alma.

Then Mama left.

Mardie and Lisbet picked up the red basket between them. Their outing was about to begin.

'Where is there a mountain?' Lisbet wanted to know.

Mardie stood on the verandah steps, thinking. There wasn't really a mountain anywhere near them and Mama had said they mustn't go too far. But Mardie didn't have to think for long, because, after all, she had ideas as fast as pigs blink. And she had remembered something. She had remembered a story which Mama had once read to them, about some children who were going to have an outing, just like Mardie and Lisbet, and they had a basket full of pancakes. But instead of going into the woods they climbed on the roof of the pigsty and all the pancakes rolled down to the pigs. That was a funny story!

'Listen, Lisbet,' said Mardie, 'we haven't got a mountain, but we can climb up on the woodshed roof.'

Lisbet jumped up and down.

'Just like those children,' she said happily. 'Only we haven't got any pancakes.'

'No, nor pigs,' said Mardie. 'So it doesn't matter if we drop our basket.'

'Do you think Mama would let us?' asked Lisbet.

Mardie thought about it.

30

'Mama said we should go to some nice place which wasn't too far away. The woodshed roof *is* a nice place, I think, and we'll have a view as well. Just like we're going to have on Wednesday.'

Just then Alma came running out.

'Where are you going?' she asked. 'I have to know.'

'Not far,' said Mardie. 'We're going to stay at home.'

Lisbet giggled.

'Not far at all. We're going . . .'

'Quiet,' said Mardie. 'I just *said* we were going to stay at home.'

Alma thought that was a good idea. She could go on with the ironing.

There was a ladder by the woodshed which Mardie had often used to get on to the roof. She liked to do a balancing act up there, right to the end of the wash-room, because the Nilssons had a pear tree with branches reaching over the washroom roof and Mardie was fond of small, juicy pears.

Lisbet had also climbed the ladder, but only the lowest rungs. Now she had to go right up and sit on the roof, it was wonderful, and awful, but that was what outings were like, Lisbet thought. Mardie climbed up first, carrying the basket. Even so, she went quickly and easily. Lisbet climbed cautiously up behind her, going more and more slowly the higher she climbed. But at last she had her nose above the roof ridge and could see Mardie up there beginning to unpack all the good food. But Lisbet didn't think the roof was a nice place any longer. She suddenly realized that a mountain would be much better.

'Mardie, do you know what?' she said. 'I don't want

31

to get on this roof.'

'Don't make a fuss, or we shan't have an outing,' said Mardie. 'Come on, I'll help you.'

Lisbet was so frightened that she was trembling, but Mardie pulled and tugged and finally succeeded in dragging her onto the roof, although Lisbet was complaining all the time:

'You're potty, Mardie, you're defuntly potty.'

Not until they were sitting astride the roof ridge with the basket between them did Lisbet begin to enjoy herself.

'Look, I can see right into the Nilssons' kitchen,' she said. Mardie nodded happily.

'Yes, what did I say? You have a view . . . you can see exactly what the Nilssons are doing. I've done it lots of times.'

They sat there for a long time, just watching the Nilssons. There was Abe, at the stove as usual. There was no sign of Mrs Nilsson, but Mr Nilsson was asleep on the kitchen sofa.

'He's probably drunk,' said Mardie, 'he usually is on Saturdays.'

Abe looked up and saw them and stopped cooking at once. Instead he went over to the window and began to make the most horrible faces which made them shriek with laughter. Mardie didn't know how anyone could twist his face up the way Abe did. He was usually handsome, Mardie thought, with his very fair hair and light blue eyes and wide mouth, yes, Abe was handsome. But just now he was screwing up his face and looking like a gnome. He wasn't handsome any more, but he was so funny that they almost rolled off the roof when they looked at him. After a little

32

while he came outside.

'Hello!' he said, looking up at Mardie and Lisbet. 'Getting on all right are you?'

'Yes, we're getting on very all right,' said Mardie.

There was nothing nicer than sitting on the wood-shed roof talking to Abe!

'We're having an outing,' Lisbet explained, to make quite sure.

'Yes, so I see,' said Abe. 'What have you got in that basket?'

'Meatballs and chipolatas and all sorts of nice things,' said Mardie.

'Very good indeed,' said Lisbet.

Abe leaned over the fence between Junedale and *Repose*, as the Nilssons' place was called. He stood there silently, looking thoughtful.

'Shall we have a bet?' he said at last. 'Shall we have a bet that you can't chuck a meatball straight into my mouth however hard you try?'

Mardie and Lisbet shouted with pleasure. No one but Abe could think of so many nice things to do.

'Ha ha, you'll see,' said Mardie, picking up a meatball at once. She aimed carefully and lobbed it down towards the open mouth. But the meatball hit Abe right on the forehead. Then it fell to the ground and finished up on a bed of golden autumn leaves. Abe whipped it up and stuffed it in his mouth.

'What did I say! You can't throw straight, you've just proved it.'

'That's odd,' said Mardie, picking up the next meatball. 'Now you'll see!'

That meatball whizzed close by Abe's ear and also fell to the ground. Abe picked it up and put it in his

mouth.

'Yes, well, you've proved it now,' he said. 'You can't throw straight, Mardie.'

'It's my turn,' said Lisbet. 'I want to throw meatballs too.'

She tossed one out without aiming and it didn't even reach the fence.

'Both of you are just as bad,' said Abe. He stuck a floury hand through the fence and raked in the meatball.

Mardie and Lisbet tried again. They tried several times, but in the end Mardie said.

'We can't have any more tries because we've finished the meatballs now.'

'Perhaps you'd do better with chipolatas,' said Abe. 'They're sort of easier to aim, why don't you try?'

Mardie and Lisbet willingly tried with chipolatas. Once Mardie succeeded in throwing a sausage right between Abe's eyes, but they never did better than that.

'Now there are only two chipolatas left,' said Mardie, 'and we'll have to have those ourselves.'

'Yes, you don't think I've got time to stand around here waiting while you practise throwing chipolatas, do you?' said Abe. 'Bye-bye, girls, you'll have to find someone else to practise on.'

Abe disappeared into his kitchen.

'Now we must have our outing,' said Lisbet. That meant she wanted to eat.

So they ate the rest of the chipolatas and the eggs and apple tart and buns. They were all very good and the girls were quite full although they had fired off all the meatballs and most of the sausages. They drank their milk as well, but Lisbet's glass wobbled and a little white stream flowed down the roof tiles to the gutter.

'Won't the sparrows be surprised when they come and see the milk in the gutter,' said Mardie.

'Yes, and pleased too,' said Lisbet. 'What shall we do now, Mardie?'

'We must go on looking at the view, because that's why you go on outings,' explained Mardie.

'Is it?' asked Lisbet.

'Yes, that's what Teacher said, and that's what we're going to do on Wednesday. Only the boys say they don't care about the view, they just want to have a good time.'

But Mardie and Lisbet were not like the boys, they looked at the view as hard as they could. Not just the Nilssons' kitchen. No, they turned their heads in all directions just as you should on outings. They could see the stream right down to the bend and the willow hanging over the water and houses and gardens along the river bank. It looked beautiful with all the red and gold autumn leaves and the sky so blue and clear. They tipped their heads back and stared at the sky too, so that they really had looked at all the view there was. They saw a bird there, hovering high, high up in the blue.

'What a view *he* must have!' said Mardie. 'I wish I could fly.'

'People can't fly,' said Lisbet.

'Yes they can, in flying machines,' said Mardie.

Abe had told her about flying machines. There were flying machines in the war but in Sweden too they had a few. Mardie would have given anything to see one, though Ida was sure that it was sinful to fly.

'I tell you, I tell you, if God wanted people to fly He would have given them wings,' said Ida.

Lisbet thought flying machines were wonderful, of course, but in fact there were other people who could fly, too.

'Do you know what, Mardie,' she said. 'The sandman can fly, just with an umbrella.'

Mardie sniffed.

'You're so childish, Lisbet.'

But suddenly Mardie began to think. Abe had said that there was someone in the war who jumped out of his flying machine with a big umbrella. Of course, Mardie realized you couldn't fly hither and thither with an umbrella like the sandman, but it seemed to be all right if you just wanted to get down to earth from a flying machine. Or . . . from some other high place! Mardie thought. The woodshed roof was a high place.

'I think I'm going to try,' said Mardie.

'What?' asked Lisbet.

'With an umbrella,' said Mardie.

When Lisbet understood what Mardie was thinking of she laughed until she cried.

'You're potty, Mardie,' she said. 'Are we going to play that you're the sandman?'

'No, of course we're not,' said Mardie. 'Don't be childish. I'm going to pretend that I'm jumping out of a flying machine, you see!'

'You're potty, Mardie,' said Lisbet again.

But the next problem was how to get Papa's big umbrella without Alma noticing. Alma might just possibly not understand about flying with an umbrella. She might begin to make a fuss because she'd never heard about what they did in the war.

But Lisbet was certainly not laughing when she was left alone on the roof. Mardie comforted her.

'Oh, I'll be back soon. You can have a little look at the Nilssons meanwhile. Just sit quite still so you don't fall off.'

Then Mardie disappeared down the ladder. She peeped into the kitchen, where Alma was ironing and dripping with sweat, She had to stoke up the fire thoroughly to keep the irons hot, so the kitchen was like an oven, although the windows were open.

Alma was glad to see Mardie.

'That's good. Now I don't have to run out to keep an eye on you. How's the outing going?'

37

'Marvellous,' said Mardie.

'Where's Lisbet?' asked Alma.

'She's still on the . . . outing,' said Mardie, hurrying through to the hall before Alma could ask any more questions. There was Papa's umbrella in the umbrella stand. Mardie had just managed to grab it when Alma looked round the door.

'Is Sasso with you?' she asked.

'No,' said Mardie, trying to hide the umbrella behind her back.

'Then he must have run down to the town as usual,' said Alma. 'What do you want the umbrella for?'

'I thought . . . it might be going to rain,' said Mardie.

'Rain! Today! No, for Heaven's sake,' said Alma. 'Put the umbrella back.'

Mardie was cross. She had no time to stand around here discussing the weather when she was supposed to be out flying for the first time in her life.

'You *have* to have umbrellas with you on outings,' she said firmly. 'What if the weather changed, then where would we be?'

Alma laughed.

'Well, it's not going to change too fast for you to get on to the verandah,' she said. 'But take the umbrella if you must. Make sure it comes back again though, or your Papa will be furious.'

'Yes, yes, yes,' said Mardie impatiently, running out of the verandah door.

Everything was very quiet. You might have thought there was not a living soul in Junedale. The most extraordinary flight was about to take place and there was not a single soul to look on, besides Lisbet. Alma's kitchen window looked out in another direction. Over

38

there in *Repose*, Abe was nowhere to be seen. Mr Nilsson was still asleep on the sofa. So only Lisbet would be looking on when Mardie flew just the way they had in the war. Only Lisbet saw her standing on the very edge of the roof ridge, putting up the big black umbrella. Only Lisbet saw her raise it high over her head and prepare to jump.

'You're potty,' said Lisbet, 'you're defuntly potty.'

'Oh, it's not dangerous,' said Mardie, although she was already thinking that it was quite a long way to the ground. But if you could jump by umbrella from a flying machine which is a thousand metres up in the air, surely to goodness you could do it from a wood-shed roof!

She stood for a time with the umbrella at full stretch, trying to sound like a flying machine. Abe had shown her what it was like. Of course Abe had never seen or heard a flying machine, but he still knew how it sounded. Abe knew everything.

'Brumm, brumm, brumm,' said Mardie.

'Oh dear,' said Lisbet.

Then Mardie flew. She stepped right out into the air. Then there was a thud.

'That was awfully quick,' called Lisbet. She wriggled forward on her tummy to the edge of the roof and looked down at Mardie. But Mardie was lying quite still with her face on the ground and did not answer. Beside her was the umbrella, with the handle snapped right off.

'What's the matter with you?' cried Lisbet. 'Are you dead?'

There was no answer this time either.

'Mardie, tell me if you're dead!' cried Lisbet anxiously.

39

But still there was no answer from Mardie. Then Lisbet began to howl her head off.

'Mama,' she howled, 'Mama!'

She seemed to be all alone in the world. And she couldn't get down from the roof, either. As she shrieked at the top of her voice, Mr Nilsson put his head out of the window.

'What are you doing up there? And what are you yelling for?'

'Mardie's dead!' screamed Lisbet. 'She's d-e-e-a-a-d!'

Mr Nilsson climbed quickly out of the window and jumped over the fence. He fell to his knees on the grass beside Mardie and turned her pale face towards him. There was blood on her forehead.

At that moment Alma came running out. She stopped dead when she caught sight of Mardie and

40

started an awful, wailing cry.

'What in all the world has happened?'

Mr Nilsson nodded mournfully.

'It's all over,' he said heavily. 'It's all over for Junedale's little Mardie!'

4
A very jolly, sad day

Mardie was lying in bed with a bandage round her head, She was not allowed to move.

'Only when you have to be sick,' said Lisbet, 'then you're allowed to move a little bit.'

Mardie was not dead and Lisbet was glad about that. She just had concussion, which is not so bad. It makes you sick, but you don't die, was what Mr Berglund said, and he was a doctor.

But there had been a great stir all over Junedale when Mardie went flying and lay on the ground and wouldn't wake up for a long time. Mama cried and Papa cried, though not as much as Mama, and Alma cried worse than Mama and Papa put together.

'It's my fault,' said Alma. 'But how was I to guess she'd taken the umbrella to fly with?'

Now Mardie was in bed and could not remember at all how it had felt to fly, wasn't that annoying? So in a way she had flown for nothing. And on top of that she had this wretched concussion, She would have to stay in bed for at least four days, Doctor Berglund said.

Mardie gave a howl when Mama told her.

'Four days . . . that's no good at all! We've got an outing on Wednesday and I'm going to . . .'

'You're not going to at all,' said Mama. 'You've had more than enough of an outing.'

Lisbet nodded agreement.

'You've had more than enough of an outing! Now you've just got to lie there and be sick.'

Then Mardie started the Great Earthquake. That was what Papa called it when she became as furious and desperate as only Mardie could be. The tears spurted from her eyes and she shrieked so that she could be heard all over the house:

'I *will* go! I *must* go! Oh, I wish I was dead!'

Lisbet gazed at her with interest and tried to comfort her.

'In my school *all* the children have concussion and can't go on any outings *at all*.'

Mama also tried to calm Mardie down.

'If you cry like that it will only make your head hurt more.'

'I don't care,' screamed Mardie. 'I wish I was dead!'

Mama looked upset then and went away. Ida was

down in the kitchen helping Alma to cook apples. When she heard the wild screams she went up to the nursery and looked sternly at Mardie.

'I tell you, I tell you, now you're being ungodly, Mardie! Remember your Maker in the days of your youth, it says in the scriptures; it does, so don't you lie here and wish your life away!'

But Mardie didn't want to think about anything except the outing and she screamed at Ida:

'Leave me alone!'

Ida shook her head sadly. 'I see, so that's how it is,' 'Solomon Grundy's come to stay, so I see!'

Solomon Grundy was bad. He came to stay, according to Ida, when Mardie and Lisbet were not as nice as Ida thought they should be. You might think it was Mardie lying there in bed, screaming, but that was only how it looked. In actual fact it was Solomon Grundy, and the real, nice Mardie hid up the chimney until Solomon Grundy decided to go away.

'It was unlucky that he decided to come just today,' said Ida.

'No, I think it's a good thing,' said Lisbet. 'Because then *he* can have a pain in his head and be sick, and Mardie can sit in the chimney and have a good time.'

But Mardie glared sourly at Lisbet and Ida. That nonsense about Solomon Grundy might be all right for Lisbet, but Mardie was too big for such childishness.

'See, now you must calm down a bit,' said Ida. 'Be glad you're alive, Mardie, you very nearly left us.'

But Mardie was not glad. She pulled the covers over her head and cried. And every morning when she woke up she hoped that a miracle would happen so that Mama would come in and say something like this:

44

'Well, well, a little concussion, what's that? In any case they say that *outings* are just the thing for concussion . . . you surely don't think you're going to miss going out on Wednesday, do you?'

But Mama said nothing of the sort. She just smiled encouragingly and patted Mardie on the cheek.

'Don't be too upset,' she said. 'We'll think of something else that's fun.'

Something else! As if anything else in all the world was more fun than the outing!

On Tuesday evening Mardie prayed to God to help her. She lay under the covers, whispering so that Lisbet should not hear her:

'Dear God, help me! I do so much want to go. Make Doctor Berglund ring Mama up and tell her that I'm well now, because I *am*. But he'll have to hurry if we're going to get it all arranged. I'm supposed to take sandwiches and chocolate and Alma has to iron my new sailor suit. So tell Doctor Berglund to ring now, right away, please, dear God, because I do so much want to go, Amen!'

Then Mardie lay listening tensely for the telephone to ring. But she heard nothing except Lisbet asking again and again from her bed:

'Tell me about ghosts and murderers and war!'

But Mardie didn't want to tell stories. She lay there for a long time listening for the telephone call which never came, then she cried a little under the covers and then she fell asleep.

On Wednesday morning she woke up early. The sun was shining out there and the sky was blue, what a lovely day for all the lucky schoolchildren who did not have concussion. She took a quick look at the clock. It would soon be eight That was when the train was leaving. They would all be gathered at the station, all her school friends, she could see them now, laughing and talking and clambering into the carriages and pushing for window seats and having fun as they waited for the train to go puffing away.

Mardie stared bitterly at the clock which was a cuckoo clock hanging on the wall above her bed. She saw the minute hand moving and heard the clock ticking its way towards eight. Then the cuckoo came out and called. Eight sneering calls it gave, and Mardie cried, because now she knew that the train had left. And here she lay and would never, never have any fun again.

Lisbet woke up in bed, in high spirits. She had no idea what a sad day this was. She was even singing:

> '*A B C D*,
> *The cat is on the spree.*
> *The cat is on the spree, my dove,*
> *For nothing else but love*'.

she sang, just as Mardie had taught her. But Mardie growled:

'Be quiet, stupid child, be quiet, be quiet!'

'I see, so that's the way it is. Solomon Grundy's come to stay,' said Lisbet, feeling like Ida.

But just then the door opened and Mama came in. She had a tray in her hands and it looked extremely grand. There were two big blue cups on it and a jug of chocolate and a plate of freshly-baked waffles.

Lisbet opened her eyes wide.

'Is it my birthday?' she asked.

'No,' said Mama. 'But you can have fun sometimes without a birthday. Sit up, Mardie, and have some chocolate and waffles.'

Mardie crawled out slowly from under the eider-down. Her eyes were wet. Mama kissed her on the cheek and served her with chocolate and waffles. Mardie began to eat without a word. She sat there quite silently, eating one waffle after another. There were still tears on her eyelashes and it was still a sad day, but waffles and chocolate are very good.

'It tastes exactly like an ordinary birthday,' she said.

'Yes, I can well believe it,' said Mama, as she left the room.

Lisbet had soon finished. She licked all the sugar and cream off her fingers and climbed determinedly out of bed. She was going to dress now. She was just finishing when the door bell rang downstairs.

'That's the postman,' said Lisbet. 'Do you want me to go and see if there's anything for us, Mardie?'

Now there was very seldom any post for Lisbet and Mardie, though for safety's sake they looked in the postbox every morning. But this time Mardie shrug-ged her shoulders. This was a sad day, so why should there be anything in the post?

Lisbet ran off all the same. Mardie was left alone and could go on thinking about the outing. She looked at the clock . . . the train journey was over and now all her class mates would be walking along the road, singing. She could see them quite clearly, marching two by two, soon they would reach the mountain where they would eat their sandwiches. And here she lay and would never have any fun, ever again!

Then Lisbet came running up the stairs, quite breathless.

'You'll never guess, Mardie,' she called, 'you've got

three cards and a parcel.'

'Have I?' said Mardie, sitting up eagerly in bed.

Both Mardie and Lisbet collected postcards and both their albums were almost full. You can get the most wonderful cards when it's your birthday. Sometimes there are flowers on them and sometimes little kittens or puppies and sometimes solemn bearded men holding ladies in beautiful dresses. A lot of cards are shiny and those are the best of all. Now Mardie had no less than three shiny cards at once, although it was not her birthday – she only had concussion. Mardie's face turned pink all over when she saw her cards – how pretty they were! On the first there was a white dove with a red rose in its beak; on the second a pink angel floating down from a dark blue sky, full of shining gold stars; and on the third there was a little boy in velvet with a bunch of yellow roses on his lap. Mardie looked at all of them and sighed with happiness. She actually had a lump in her throat – the cards were so gloriously beautiful!

'Have a look and see who they're from,' Lisbet reminded her, and Mardie quickly turned the cards over.

'From a friend,' was printed on all three of them.

'What on earth does that mean?' said Mardie.

Cards were usually from Grandmama or from cousins, not from a friend. It was something quite new and extraordinary to get cards from someone without knowing who it was.

'Perhaps it's Abe,' suggested Lisbet.

'Sending three cards?' said Mardie. 'He's not crazy, you know!'

She was so pleased with her cards that she almost

48

forgot the parcel. But now she was in a hurry to undo it. There was a box inside and in the box there was a lot of pink tissue paper. Mardie and Lisbet looked at each other, quivering with excitement. There might be absolutely anything under that pink paper and it was marvellous not knowing what it was. Mardie bent over it and sniffed.

'What do you think it can be?'

Lisbet sniffed as well.

'I don't know.'

'Do you think I should look?' asked Mardie.

'Defuntly,' said Lisbet.

The tissue paper rustled under Mardie's eager fingers. Lisbet held her breath.

There was a letter on top. '*To Mardie from Grandmama*' it said on the envelope. But Grandmama had not only sent a letter, not at all! There was a tiny, tiny baby doll and a tiny, tiny bathtub for the doll to bath in and a tiny, tiny bottle for the doll to suck from and a tiny, tiny towel for her to dry with. And then there was a little box of beads for making necklaces and two little green gift boxes with a pretty picture on the lid and pink sugar sweets and a beautiful ring inside.

Lisbet's eyes were round as she looked at all the things Mardie had been sent. She became more and more thoughtful and at last she said gloomily:

'I want to have concussion too!'

Mardie picked up the gift boxes, one in each hand.

'Which would you like?' she asked. 'Would you rather have a ring with a red stone in, or one with a blue stone in?'

'The green one,' said Lisbet.

49

'There isn't a green one, silly,' said Mardie.

'Then I want the blue one,' said Lisbet. 'Oh, you are kind, Mardie!'

Mardie thought she was kind too. It felt good. And it felt good not to be sad any more and to be able to stop thinking about the outing.

'Mountains can be all right,' she told Lisbet. 'But in any case, I think we had a better view from the woodshed roof.'

'Defuntly,' said Lisbet. 'We could see right into the Nilssons' kitchen.'

Mardie and Lisbet put on their rings, spread out their fingers and felt like fine ladies.

'My stone looks like a drop of blood,' said Mardie. 'What does yours look like, Lisbet?'

'Mine looks like blue,' said Lisbet, 'and it is, too.'

They compared rings for a long time. They put their hands side by side and wondered which ring was the prettiest. It turned out that Mardie thought red stones were prettiest because they looked like drops of blood and Lisbet thought blue stones were prettiest because they were blue.

'Oh dear, I haven't read the letter from Grandmama,' Mardie remembered suddenly, and she opened the envelope quickly.

Grandmama had written in printed letters because Mardie couldn't read joined up letters yet. Lisbet couldn't understand how Mardie could make out what Grandmama meant, just by looking at a few small squiggles in a letter.

'Can you really read it?' she asked.

And of course Mardie could. When she had spelled her way through the letter she knew exactly what

Grandmama said. She said that Mardie must give up flying altogether and that she should give Lisbet one of the gift boxes and half the beads in the bead box.

'Wasn't I kind, Lisbet, giving you the gift box *before* I'd read the letter?' said Mardie.

'Yes, you were kind,' said Lisbet, grabbing the bead box. 'Give me my beads, I'm going to make a necklace!'

But Mardie snatched the bead box out of her hand.

'Let go,' she said, 'you have to wait till I've got time to divide them up.'

'You've got time *now*,' said Lisbet.

'No, I haven't,' said Mardie.

She picked up the carafe which stood on the table beside the bed and poured out some water for herself. Then she drank it in slow, small gulps until the glass was empty. Then she picked up the pink tissue paper and began to fold it very tidily. She folded and folded, so that anyone could see she had more important things to do than counting beads. All the time she was thinking. A gift box is really nicer than a bead box, thought Mardie, but it was easier to give the gift box to Lisbet than divide the beads with her. Mardie knew that she would have liked to keep the whole box for herself, but she realised that if Lisbet did not get any beads, she would go to Mama and tell tales and then Mardie would be forced to divide them up anyway.

Mardie put the tissue paper back in the box as tidily and carefully as she could and then she said with a sigh:

'Now I've got time.'

She emptied the beads onto a tray and divided them fairly into two piles. But she had one big yellow bead

51

left over, which she gave to Lisbet.

'You can have this,' she said, because Mardie was never mean for more than a short time.

Then Mardie and Lisbet made themselves necklaces and became even grander than before. They played with the baby doll and bathed her in the little bathtub and dried her with the little towel which smelled so good. And then they put her to bed in a cigar box and gave her the bottle to suck.

'This is really a sad day,' said Mardie, 'only actually it's great fun.'

Lisbet agreed with her.

'Yes, it's a very jolly, sad day,' she said.

But in the end Lisbet got bored and wanted to go out.

'I must go for a walk with Sasso,' she said, and in a flash she was gone.

It is no fun playing alone. Mardie was very bored and did not know what to do next. But then Papa came home for lunch. He came up to the nursery for a while.

'How do you feel?' he asked.

'Marvellous,' said Mardie. 'But I haven't got anything to do.'

'You can read the paper if you like,' said Papa, pulling a newspaper out of his pocket. 'Here's a drawing pad too, so make me a nice drawing for when I come home at suppertime.'

Mardie had learned to read so quickly that even Teacher had been surprised and when Papa had gone she immediately opened the newspaper. But she could not understand very much of what was in it. It was mostly about the war and then there were advertisements about pigs and oxen for sale and notices of

people who were dead and engaged and about elegant ladies' clothes. There were a great many other things as well, but only boring things. Mardie read the headings suspiciously. '*From Bygone Days*' she read – could that possibly be amusing? Mardie didn't know what 'Bygone Days' were, but she soon found out. It was about what people had done in the past, poor people, what a boring time they must have had! Mardie sighed and put the newspaper down. It was very odd that Papa, who was so entertaining, could make such a boring paper. He was the Editor, he was the one who decided what was to be in it, why couldn't he put in some amusing things? But perhaps it was difficult to write papers . . . She could try to do one herself, then she would know, thought Mardie. Of course, it couldn't be printed, but she could write it on the drawing pad and she could cut the headings out of Papa's paper, so that it would all look almost real.

With drawing pad and pencil and scissors and glue-pot on the tray in front of her, Mardie was soon busy.

'*From Bygone Days*' was at the top of the sheet. She had cut that out of Papa's newspaper. Now she had to decide what was to go underneath it. Mardie chewed her pencil and thought. Then she wrote:

From Bygone Days

NOW I SHALL TELL YOU WAHT CHILDREN DID BEFOR. THEY WERE NISE tO THEIR MAMA BUT SOME WERE NARSTY AND NOT SO NISE. THEY HAD STONE AKSES BUT THEY SOON LERND TO SHOOT WITH GUNS.

That was all Mardie could write about bygone days. She picked up the scissors and cut a new heading out of Papa's newspaper: **'From The Front'**. She stuck it onto a fresh sheet in the drawing block and then chewed her pencil again while she thought. Then she wrote:

From The Front

ITS ORFUL IN THE WAR THE SOLJERS LIE
IN TRENCHES AND THERE FEET FREESE
BUT ONE SOLJER JUMPED DOWN WITH AN
UMBRELLA AND DIDNT GET CONCUSHION
IT WAS FROM A FLYING MASHINE.

With that Mardie had finished writing about the war. She began to look through Papa's newspaper for new ideas. Announcements . . . did you have to have them too, to make a real newspaper?

She cut out the heading **'Deaths'** and stuck it on a fresh page. Then she chewed her pencil and thought. She thought for a long time, then nodded happily and began to write.

When the announcement was finished she drew a black frame round it. Then she suddenly felt that she did not want to make a newspaper any more, drawing was more fun. So she made a drawing for Papa. It showed her flying off the woodshed roof and it was very successful.

Papa was given it when he came home for supper and he liked it too. Mardie was at the supper table in her dressing-gown. Perhaps she couldn't manage to go on outings yet, but she could manage to eat mashed swedes and apple custard.

When night came Mardie and Lisbet were in their beds and ready for sleep. Mama and Papa came to the nursery for a little goodnight visit . . . Mama told them the story of Prince Hatt who lived under the ground, and Papa made shadow pictures for them on the wall. The oil-lamp in the nursery, shed a very gentle light but Papa took off the globe so that the light was stronger and the shadow pictures looked beautiful. They moved on the wall; sometimes you could see a billy-goat with two horns, sometimes a girl dancing, and sometimes just the shadow of Papa's hand and nothing else.

It was fun having Mama and Papa in the nursery at the same time. Mardie wished she could keep them there for a long, long time. At last Mama said:

'Well, it's high time you were asleep!'

And Lisbet was actually asleep already. But Mardie lay awake for a long time that night. She was thinking about the outing again. Of course it was over now, but still! The day after tomorrow she was going to school and she knew what all her classmates would be talking about. Nothing but what fun, what absolutely extraordinary fun they had had. But not Mardie. Oh, why had she not been allowed to go?

The stars were very big in the sky that night. She could see a whole lot of them through the gap in the blind. They were almost as beautiful as the stars on her angel card. She tried to count them but it was difficult. Counting stars makes you sleepy.

Now the whole of Junedale was falling asleep by its peaceful stream and among its white birches. In the dark house no one was awake but Mama. Soon she too would be asleep but first she would pay a visit to the nursery to tuck her little girls in.

She cast the light of her little green night-lamp over Lisbet's bed. Lisbet was lying on her tummy as usual. All you could see of her was a brown neck and a mass of fair curly hair. When Mama bent over her she muttered in her sleep:

'You're potty, Mardie!'

Then Mama went over to her big girl, but her big girl looked very small when she was sleeping. Small and sweet, with her lashes dark against her cheek. There was a piece of paper on the floor beside her bed. Mama picked it up and read it by the light of her lamp.

Deaths

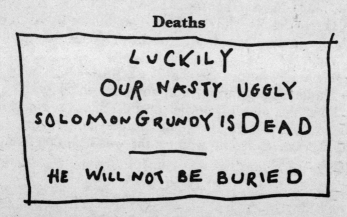

On Friday morning Mardie went to school, very unwillingly, dragging her feet. She didn't want to go and hear about the outing.

Twenty minutes later she came storming home again. She jumped, or rather flew, right into the kitchen and almost scared the life out of Mama who thought something awful must have happened, otherwise why would Mardie come home in the middle of school, looking completely wild?

'Mama,' panted Mardie, 'Mama . . . we're having an outing . . . today . . . now . . . there wasn't one on Wednesday . . . Teacher tripped on the stairs . . . Oh, I'm so happy . . . she got concussion too . . . I want chocolate in a thermos . . . where's my sailor suit, quick, Mama, quick!'

When Ida came to do the Friday cleaning a little later, she met Mardie at the gate. Mardie in her new sailor suit, with a sailor hat on her head, oh, how she was beaming, and how the rucksack danced on her back as she gave excited little leaps!

'I'm going on an outing,' said Mardie, 'I'm so happy!'

'I see,' said Ida. 'Weren't you the one who was lying screaming and wishing she were dead? I suppose you're singing another tune today.'

'Ha ha,' said Mardie, 'that was Solomon Grundy who wished he was dead. And he is, too. It was in the newspaper.'

'What newspaper was that?' asked Ida.

'Ha ha,' said Mardie, 'I'm not going to tell you.'

Then she went off on her outing. She was going to go by train, and she was going to sit on a mountain and eat sandwiches, so no wonder she was beaming as she went.

5
Lisbet sticks a pea up her nose

It was autumn now and every Thursday they had pea-
soup at Junedale. Lisbet didn't stick a pea up her nose
every Thursday, she did it only once. She liked
sticking things into things where they were not supposed to be. She stuck the key to the maid's room in
the letter box, she pushed Mama's ring into her piggy-
bank so that it was impossible to get it out without
breaking the pig, she managed to work Papa's cycle
clips into an empty bottle. She didn't do it from
naughtiness but just to see what happened. It's fun
to find out if things will go in to places where you don't
think they can. Now she had found a pea on the
kitchen floor and in a flash she had stuck it up her
nose. Just to see if it went in. It did. A long way in.

Then Lisbet wanted to get the pea out again. She
had finished with her test. But the pea did not want to
come out. It stayed where it was. Lisbet poked and
poked but the pea would not come out. Lisbet asked
Mardie to help and Mardie tried too, but no, the pea
would not come out.

'Perhaps it's taken root in there,' suggested Mardie.
'You'll see, in no time at all there'll be sweetpeas

growing out of your nostrils . . . I hope they'll smell nice, at least.'

Lisbet started to howl. She liked sweetpeas but she liked them to grow in the garden, not out of her own nose! She ran to Mama, shrieking loudly:

'Mama, I've got a pea in my nose, take it out! I don't *want* it there!'...

'Oh,' said Mama, 'oh!'

This was just the day when she had one of her bad headaches and only wanted to lie on her bed with her eyes closed, not to start digging peas out of Lisbet's nose.

'I don't *want* it there!' screamed Lisbet. 'Take it away!'

Mama got a hairpin and tried to coax the nasty pea out. She coaxed and coaxed, but it was no good. The pea stayed where it was.

'Mardie, you'll have to take Lisbet down to Doctor Berglund,' said Mama. 'He's sure to be able to get it out.'

'Are you sure he can?' asked Lisbet.

'Quite sure,' said Mama. Then she lay down on her bed again. Her head was very painful.

'Come on, Mardie, let's hurry,' said Lisbet. She had no idea how quickly sweetpeas might grow and it would be awful if they started shooting out as they walked down the street. Lisbet was afraid people might laugh at her. But Mardie comforted her. If a sweetpea really should happen to grow, it would not be such a great misfortune.

'You can cut it off so that no one can see it, and put it in your buttonhole,' said Mardie.

Lisbet was not one to go on grumbling for long, over a mere trifle like a pea. Now she was on the way to the doctor, the pea was almost as good as gone, and after all, it wasn't every day she was allowed to go into town with Mardie.

'It's going to be great fun,' said Lisbet. 'Come on, Mardie!'

It was a long way to Doctor Berglund's house. He lived on the main square in the middle of the town and Junedale was on the outskirts.

Mardie held Lisbet firmly by the hand. Mama would have been pleased to see how nicely they were walking along.

'You do some silly things,' said Mardie, feeling

62

grown-up and wise. She had quite forgotten who got up to most of the silly things in their family. But it certainly was fun to be going in to town; Mardie thought so too, so Lisbet was not scolded any more.

The street was covered with dry leaves. When you kicked them they made a lovely rustling sound. Mardie and Lisbet ploughed through the piles of leaves, kicking them as hard as they could. They swung their arms and their cheeks turned red. The weather was fresh and cool and in the gardens all the flowers were black and withered. It comforted Lisbet . . . she could see now that the time for flowers was over, there would be no sweetpeas just now.

'Shall we go in and say hello to Ida?' suggested Mardie. 'We'll be going near there.'

'Oh yes, we could do that,' said Lisbet. It was a long time since she'd been to see Ida and the pea might as well stay there a bit longer.

Mardie and Lisbet liked Ida and they liked her little house almost more. She had the smallest house in town; the roof was so low that Ida could only just stand up straight. She had only a small room and a tiny, tiny kitchen, but they were beautiful. Ida had flowers in the window and two wonderful, terrible pictures on the wall above her bed, and she had an open hearth on which she would bake apples for Mardie and Lisbet. So it would be silly not to drop in on her, since they were actually going past.

Mardie and Lisbet were just about to knock on the door when they saw that Ida had left a note on it. '*Back in a moment*' it said. Ida was not at home. Fortunately Mardie and Lisbet were not in too much, of a hurry to wait a bit. And the door wasn't locked so they could just walk in.

It was marvellously cosy in Ida's house. They warm-
ed themselves by the glow from the open hearth and
looked at the awful pictures over Ida's bed. There was
a mountain spouting fire in one of them. Mardie and
Lisbet shivered to see the poor people in the picture
running to escape the fire. What a good thing there
were no fire-spitting mountains in Sweden! The other
picture was equally dreadful. There were lots of men
just about to be drowned in a flood; oh, how frightened
they were and how they longed to get ashore! But
the river was rushing so wildly that the only thing to
come out was a little bottle, lying on the ground.
'*Will you also drown in a flood of brandy*' it said under the
picture. Mardie and Lisbet shuddered. No, they were
certainly going to take care that they didn't get into
any brandy floods.

'They're the best pictures I've seen in my life,' said
Mardie.

'Defuntly,' said Lisbet.

Then they looked at the photographs of Esther and
Ruth who were Ida's children. The photographs
had come from America, which was where Ruth and
Esther lived. They were fine ladies, with beautiful,
flowery clothes and their hair piled up in a birds'
nest on their heads. Their photographs stood on Ida's
desk but they themselves were in Chicago and would
never come home again.

Beside the desk hung Ida's guitar. Mardie began to
twang the strings, it sounded lovely. Oh, Mardie
would have given anything in the world to play as
Ida played. But Lisbet was not interested in music.
She stood by the window looking out, to see if there

64

was anything interesting in the garden. There was. There were a couple of dustbins and a little square of lawn and a big tree and round the garden a row of small houses almost like Ida's. But all that was not particularly interesting. The interesting thing was the red-headed girl sitting on the steps of one of the houses. The girl must be Mattie, whom Ida had told them about, and Lisbet was very anxious to go and talk to her.

'I'll be back soon,' she told Mardie. But as Mardie had taken down the guitar and was playing it, she could neither hear nor see. She played one note at a time and at each note she closed her eyes and listened. She could hear it ringing round the room and it made her happy.

Lisbet was already out in the garden. There was Mattie, sitting in front of her house. She had a knife in her hand and was whittling a piece of wood. She pretended not to have seen Lisbet. Lisbet approached her slowly and stopped at a distance, as you do if you have elegant manners. She stood there quietly, waiting for Mattie to look up. 'Snotty nose,' said Mattie briefly and forcefully, and went on chipping away at the piece of wood.

Lisbet was angry. If *anyone* had a snotty nose and ought to blow it, it was Mattie.

'Snotty nose yourself, dirty pig,' said Lisbet. She was quite scared when she had said that. True, Mattie was no bigger than she was, but she looked so determined and dangerous.

'Would you like me to stick my knife into you?' asked Mattie.

Lisbet had no answer to that. She took a couple of

65

steps back and then put out her tongue. Mattie put out her tongue too and then she said:

'I've got two rabbits, sucks to you, you haven't!'

Lisbet had never before heard the expression 'sucks to you', but she realised that if Mattie said sucks to you, it would be something scoffing, and Lisbet was not slow to learn a good new word.

'I've got a kitten called Goodie, sucks to you, you haven't,' she said.

'Ha ha, it's teeming with cats here, we're sick to death of them,' said Mattie. 'I wouldn't *want* a kitten, even if you threw one at me!'

There was a moment's silence while Mattie and Lisbet glared furiously at each other. Then Mattie said:

'I've had an appendix operation, so I've got a big scar on my tummy, sucks to you, you haven't!'

That was enough for Lisbet. She thought quickly. Had she anything to compare with a scar on the tummy? Yes, of course she had!

'I've got a pea in my nose, sucks to you, you haven't!'

But Mattie laughed scornfully.

'Peas, I've got enough peas to stuff my nose full. What's funny about that?'

Lisbet felt awkward and mumbled:

'If it was to grow into a sweetpea . . .'

She said it very quietly, because what was there to boast about in a sweetpea you didn't want?

But Mattie sat there wiping her nose on her sleeve and when Lisbet saw that, she remembered something useful.

'You know what,' she said, 'you couldn't stuff your

nose full of peas because you've got such a snotty nose!'

Then Mattie was really angry.

'I'll give you snotty nose,' she shrieked, rushing at Lisbet. Lisbet thrashed around with her arms and defended herself as best as she could, but Mattie was very strong. She punched and hit and cuffed Lisbet and pushed her against the wall. Lisbet screamed for all she was worth.

'Mardie! Mardie!'

There was no need for Lisbet to put up with such treatment when she had a sister like Mardie. Mardie knew how to fight! When she was angry – and she got angry very easily – she did not really know what she was doing. She just jumped right in with both feet. It was no good Mama telling her off. Little girls mustn't fight, Mama said, but Mardie never remembered that until afterwards and by then it was too late. She generally regretted it and decided never to fight again, but if someone was attacking her little sister that was more than she could bear. And now she came tearing out of the door like a goat from its stall. Before Mattie could blink she had received a blow which made her tumble over backwards.

'Sucks to you!' said Lisbet.

But Mattie had a sister too.

'Mia,' shrieked Mattie, 'Mia!'

And who should come tearing out of the nearest house like a goat from its stall but Mia, Mardie's classmate, the one with all those nits in her hair.

Mattie howled and pointed at Mardie.

'She hit me so I fell over!'

'Dirty pig, you started it,' Lisbet tried to explain, but it was no use. Mardie and Mia were already at it, hammer and tongs. Mia was small and tough and fiery, she pinched and scratched and pulled hair. Mardie didn't, she fought like a boy and wrestled and she was strong. Soon Mia was on her back on the ground and could not scratch any more, because Mardie was sitting right on top of her, holding her arms in a firm grip.

'Do you give up?' asked Mardie.

Then Mia said something terrible.

'Not to you, you little devil.'

Mardie and Lisbet gazed at her, appalled. You could say snotty-nose, you could say dirty pig, but you couldn't say devil, that was swearing. And people who swear go to Hell, Ida had told them that.

Poor Mia! Mardie was so sorry for her that she let go of her arms. You can't fight with someone who's

got to go to Hell. Then Mia quickly brought up her
fist and thumped Mardie right on the nose. It wasn't
a very hard blow, but it was enough for Mardie to
start a nose bleed. She often had one and it had never
worried Lisbet before. But now she saw the blood
pouring from Mardie's nose, she screamed as if it
were her life's blood.

'Mardie's dead!' she screamed. 'Mardie's dead!'

Then a guardian angel appeared . . . Ida!

'I tell you, I tell you, you're stark, raving mad, it's
plain to see!'

She grabbed hold of Mia and Mardie with her hard
fists and pulled them apart.

'Is that any way to behave? Aren't you ashamed?'

Mardie and Lisbet began to be ashamed at once. Not so Mia and Mattie. They were just as cheeky as before. They certainly withdrew hastily to their own house, but they stood staring out of the door and pulling long faces at Mardie and Lisbet. Dusk was falling, but Mardie and Lisbet could still see their mops of red hair and their scornful grins.

'Snotty noses should be given what for!' shouted Mia, and Mattie added:

'Come here and we'll give you what for, the two of you!'

'I tell you, I tell you,' muttered Ida, 'them there children will end up in prison one fine day.'

Fighting makes you tired. Both Mardie and Lisbet really had to go in with Ida and have a rest. Ida scolded them and grumbled. Look at Mardie, the blood was running out of her nose and her nice dark blue coat was grey with dirt and dust. But Ida gave her a damp cloth to put over her nose and brushed her coat so that it looked neat again. Then she put more wood on the fire and they sat in front of the hearth, baking apples, while Ida played the guitar and sang to them.

'More, more,' said Mardie and Lisbet every time Ida tried to stop. So she sang a whole lot of sad songs for them, such as *The North Wind Doth Blow And We Shall Have Snow* and *Old Man River* and *Lord Ullin's Daughter*, Finally she sang *Jesus Railway To The Sky*, but then Mardie put the damp cloth over her eyes instead.

'Ha ha, that's just so we won't see you're crying,' said Lisbet.

70

She herself never cried at any song, however sad it was.

Now Ida was putting down her guitar.

'You'd better go home now,' she said, 'otherwise Mama may be beginning to wonder where you've got to.'

That was when Mardie remembered. The pea! The doctor! Oh dear, oh dear, she had forgotten all about it.

'Hurry up, Lisbet, come on, let's run, here . . . put

on your coat, hurry up!'

Ida was very surprised.

'I didn't mean to drive you out quite so suddenly,' she said.

But Mardie and Lisbet were not listening to her. With scarcely a goodbye they ran out without even buttoning their coats. Five minutes later they were ringing at Doctor Berglund's door. Mardie had run herself into another nose bleed by then and when Doctor Berglund opened the door he stepped back before the awful face which met his eyes.

'Save us,' he said, 'have you been fighting?'

'Does it show?' asked Mardie.

'Yes,' said Doctor Berglund, and he was speaking the truth. Mardie's nose had swollen up and looked like a glowing red potato in the middle of her face. She no longer looked like Mardie, she looked like someone else altogether. Doctor Berglund swept them in to his reception room.

'Actually I thought it was Lisbet who was to be the patient this time,' he said. 'That was what your Mama said, in any case.'

'Did Mama ring up?' asked Mardie anxiously.

'Yes, but only three times,' said Doctor Berglund.

'Oh dear,' said Mardie.

'Oh dear,' said Lisbet.

'She was wondering what had become of you,' said Doctor Berglund. 'She was wondering if you were still alive.'

'Yes, of course we're alive,' mumbled Mardie shamefacedly.

Doctor Berglund sat her down on a chair and stuffed two big tufts of cottonwool up her nostrils.

72

That made Lisbet laugh till she shook.

'You look potty, Mardie,' she said, 'you look like a snail with two little white horns in front.'

But then Lisbet stopped talking, because Doctor Berglund had taken out a funny little hook, which he stuck up her nose. It didn't hurt but it tickled terribly. First he put the hook up the right nostril and then up the left and then up the right again.

'Can you remember which nostril you poked the pea into?' asked Doctor Berglund.

'This one,' said Lisbet, pointing to the left nostril.

So Doctor Berglund pushed the hook up again and dug about until it tickled even worse than before.

'That's odd,' he said at last, 'I can't find a pea.'

'No, of course not,' said Lisbet. 'The pea flew out when I was fighting Mattie, you see!'

That night Mardie and Lisbet could not go to sleep. So much had happened that day which they needed to talk about after they were in bed.

Of course they were in a bit of trouble when they got home, but it wasn't too bad. Mama was glad that they had not disappeared altogether and all Papa said was:

'Now then, you girls, a kiss and a smack and off to bed and to sleep!'

But Mardie and Lisbet were only kissed, not smacked, and they didn't go to sleep either, although the lamp in the nursery had been put out long before.

'Can I come in your bed?' asked Lisbet.

'Yes, if you take care you don't bang my nose,' said Mardie.

'Can I lie on your arm?' Lisbet asked, and she

could. Mardie liked having Lisbet lying on her arm. It felt as if she were very big and Lisbet very small and it felt warm in a special way.

'That Mattie ought to get what for,' said Lisbet . . . she had learned so many good new words today.

'Mia ought to get what for, too,' said Mardie.

'Defuntly,' said Lisbet. 'Is she that stupid at school, too?'

'Not quite,' said Mardie. 'But she is rather silly. Can you guess what she said once, when Teacher was going to hear our Bible lesson?'

Lisbet couldn't guess.

'It was about when God made the first people, you know. In the Garden of Eden, you know. Mia was supposed to say what He did and can you guess what she said?'

No, Lisbet still couldn't guess.

'She said: "God made the man fall into a heavy sleep and then He took a ribbon and created the woman from it."'

'Wasn't that what He did?' asked Lisbet.

'Oh, you're as silly as Mia. He didn't take a ribbon at all.'

'What did He take, then?' asked Lisbet.

'A rib, of course!'

'Where did He get the rib from?' asked Lisbet.

'Oh, how should I know? It doesn't say that in the Bible. I suppose Adam must have been having it for dinner before he went to sleep.'

Lisbet thought about the question of the rib for some time, then she said:

'Mia ought to get what for. A ribbon, ha ha, isn't she silly!'

They agreed that Mia was silly. But suddenly Mardie remembered the terrible word Mia had said and she felt quite miserable all of a sudden. Of course she thought Mia should get what for, but oh, if she had to go to Hell, just because Lisbet had stuck a pea up her nose! It was all the fault of that wretched pea! But for the pea they would never have gone to Ida's house and there wouldn't have been a fight and Mia would never have said that terrible word. Mardie explained this to Lisbet.

'Oh dear, oh dear,' said Lisbet.

They lay there, stricken with horror, wondering what to do.

'Perhaps it would help if we asked God to forgive Mia,' said Mardie. 'I don't believe she'll ever do it herself.'

Mardie and Lisbet folded their hands, because after all, they had to do what they could to save Mia.

'Dear kind God, forgive Mia just this once, forgive her, forgive her!'

And Mardie added:

'Dear God, perhaps she didn't mean it. In any case I'm not sure she really said "little devil" . . . I think perhaps she just said "little girl".'

She felt better after that. They had saved Mia from eternal damnation, and now it was time to sleep.

Lisbet tiptoed back to her own bed. Mardie felt her nose cautiously. It did feel a little smaller now and that was good.

'Actually it's been a really nice day today,' said Mardie. 'And that was because of the pea too, when you come to think of it.'

'So it was a good thing I poked it in after all,' said Lisbet. 'When you come to think of it.'

'Yes,' said Mardie. 'Only you should have poked one up the other nostril too, and we might have had twice as much fun, ha ha?'

But by then Lisbet was falling asleep and was not in the mood for jokes.

'Do you know what, Mardie,' she said sleepily. 'In my school the children have only *one* nostril!'

Then both Lisbet and Mardie fell asleep.

6

Mardie finds out if she has 'second sight'

Mama did not really like Mardie visiting the Nilssons. Mardie herself liked nowhere better than the Nilssons' kitchen. And once she heard Papa telling Mama:

'Let her go! I want my children to know that there are different kinds of people. That way they may learn not to be too ready to take strong measures.'

Mardie was not intended to hear this, so she could not ask Papa why one should not be ready to take strong measures. Perhaps Papa meant that people should not be so angry with Mr Nilsson when he got drunk on Saturdays. Mardie wasn't angry with him because Mr Nilsson was always nice to her and called her 'Junedale's little Mardie', and he was never nasty to Abe or Mrs Nilsson either.

'When I'm at home in *Repose*, I want to repose,' said Mr Nilsson, lying down on the kitchen sofa. 'You can't just toil and sweat for wife and child, you have to take a rest sometimes!'

Mrs Nilsson knew that Mr Nilsson needed his rest. It was only sometimes that she didn't understand. When the dustmen arrived Mrs Nilsson didn't want to carry the dustbin down to the gate herself, Mr Nilsson had to do it. He didn't like that at all. Afterwards he would lie on the sofa and not speak to Mrs Nilsson for a long time. He just stared up at the ceiling and talked sadly to himself:

'Of course I'm both the house-owner and the land-owner, and yet I have to carry the dustbin right down the garden.'

But when Mr Nilsson played the gramophone and danced with Mrs Nilsson and Abe stood at the stove baking and the smell of newly-baked sugar buns spread all over *Repose*, it was very jolly in the Nilssons' kitchen. Alma, who sometimes came there to fetch Mardie, had been known to say that there was more junk and rubbish there than anywhere else she had seen in her life, but how many places had Alma seen? It might be true that the Nilssons did not sweep up often and did not wash the dishes except when it was really necessary, but all the same it was fine, Mardie thought. Mrs Nilsson had some embroidered hangings which she had sewn herself. '*A Place for Everything*' and '*Everything in its Place*' the hangings said, in red cross-stitch and the longest hangings said '*Sun outside, sun inside, sun in heart and sun in mind*'.

'Some day soon I must take them down and wash them,' said Mrs Nilsson. 'Then you'll be able to see what they say better.'

'Oh, you won't read it anyway,' said Mr Nilsson, holding Mrs Nilsson round the waist and dancing and singing:

> '*Come Adolfina*
> *Come Adolfina*
> *Hold me close.*
> *Come Adolfina,*

Come Adolfina,
Join in the waltz . . .'

'Oh, what rubbish you can talk,' said Mrs Nilsson, laughing till her tummy wobbled. And Abe stood at the stove whistling 'Come Adolfina' and turning buns to the beat.

But when Mardie and Abe were alone in the kitchen, that was the best time of all. Abe knew so much and talked so well while he was baking. Mardie sat on the kitchen sofa and listened. All the things she told Lisbet about ghosts and murderers and war she had originally heard from Abe. Abe had only met two or three murderers but he had seen plenty of ghosts. Mardie had not seen a single one.

'It's because I've got second sight,' said Abe. 'You have to have, otherwise you don't see any ghosts.'

Second sight . . . Mardie had never heard of that before, but Abe explained it to her. If you had second sight, you had special kinds of eyes which could see ghosts and spirits where ordinary people don't see anything at all. Abe himself was surprised that there could be such a difference.

'I don't understand it . . . an ordinary person can go straight through a ghost and not notice a thing.'

'Do you think I'm an ordinary person?' asked Mardie eagerly. 'Perhaps I've got second sight too, although I've never been to a place where there are ghosts.'

Abe laughed scornfully.

'Second sight, you? You've no more got second sight than a pig.'

He stood shaping his buns for a while, then he

added:

'Although, come to think of it – I could take you to
the churchyard with me one dark night and try.'

Mardie shivered.

'The churchyard . . . are there ghosts there?'

'Oh yes, there are,' said Abe. 'Of course I've seen ghosts in other places too, but in the churchyard they're as thick as asparagus stalks, shoals of them! You can scarcely walk there without bumping into some spirit.'

Mardie did want to know if she had second sight, but she did not want to go to the churchyard in the middle of the night, when the ghosts were as thick as asparagus stalks.

'Isn't there anywhere else where there aren't quite so many?' she asked.

Abe stared at her with his bright blue eyes.

'Are you a coward?'

Mardie wriggled and did not answer. It would be awful if Abe thought she was a coward, but it would be more awful to go to the churchyard in the middle of the night.

Abe looked thoughtful.

'Of course we could try somewhere else too,' he said, lobbing a bun on to the baking tray. 'Out in our wash-house, for instance; there's something haunting that like crazy!'

'Is there?' said Mardie, surprised. She had often been in the Nilssons' wash-house but had never seen a sign of a ghost or spirit . . . Did that really mean she no more had second sight than a pig?

'Not that I think it's really worth it,' said Abe, 'but we could try, just to make sure. What about tonight?'

Mardie wriggled again.

'Does it have to be at night?'

'Yes, what did you think? Did you think the ghost wanted to help Ma with the washing? Oh no, twelve o'clock at night, that's the right time for ghosts, and that's when he comes, not one minute before.'

'Why does he come to your wash-house?' asked Mardie.

Abe was silent for a time and then he said:

'You'd better hear all about it. Actually it's a secret, so you must promise not to say anything to a living soul.'

Mardie quivered with excitement. She was not one to tell secrets, Abe knew that, so, for her ears *alone*, he told the story of the ghost in the wash-house. Mardie had never heard anything so extraordinary. The ghost was none other than Abe's own great-great-grandfather, who had lived a hundred years ago and was the richest nobleman you could imagine . . . Abe himself was as good as a nobleman, although he kept it secret.

Mardie stared at him, her eyes round with astonishment. She had never heard anything like it!

'Can you understand,' said Abe, 'why my great-great-grandfather cannot rest like other dead old

noblemen? Oh no, he floats around the wash-house every night instead, and do you know why?'

Mardie didn't know, but Abe explained. Rich as that nobleman was, he had buried a whole load of money in his boathouse, which Mrs Nilsson now used as a wash-house.

'Just for fun, you know,' said Abe. 'He had stuffed the banks so chockful of money that there was no room left there, but then he thought of the boathouse. And when he had just buried the treasure, he went and died. That's why he haunts it now and can't rest.'

Mardie gasped.

'Do you mean the money's still there?'

'Of course it's still there,' said Abe.

Mardie stared at him.

'Then why don't you dig it up?'

'Dig it up yourself and see where you get,' said Abe. 'For instance, would you know where to dig?'

No, Mardie wouldn't know.

'There you are then,' said Abe.

Mardie looked at him as if she'd never seen him before. There he was, baking buns, and in actual fact he was a nobleman and had a great-great-grand-father who was also a nobleman . ... and a ghost on top of that!

'What's the ghost's name? Your great-great-grand-father, I mean?'

Abe stopped in the middle of a bun. When he answered at last, it was if he were reading from a book.

'And his name was Lord Abe Nilsson . . . Crow,' said Abe.

It sounded so fine and so frightful, that Mardie got

goose-pimples when she heard it.

'It's lucky we're not proud,' said Abe. 'The Right Honourable Lord Abe Nilsson Crow is what you should *really* call me. But never mind. You can go on saying Abe!'

'Yes, because otherwise I could never talk to you,' said Mardie. 'But I could call you the "Right Honourable Abe" *sometimes*, of you like.'

But Abe didn't like. All he wanted was Mardie to come to the wash-house at twelve o'clock. Because if it turned out that she really had second sight, she could help to corner Lord Crow . . . perhaps they would finally manage to talk to him about the money. Abe had tried several times but his great-great-grandfather just vanished through the wall with a muffled sigh.

Mardie began to wonder if this second sight business was really something worth having. Of course, she would like to see a ghost, but not if she had to chase Abe's great-great-grandfather round the wash-house at midnight.

'Mama wouldn't let me,' said Mardie. 'I would never, never be allowed to go out in the middle of the night.'

What a silly thing to say! Abe felt sorry for Mardie.

'Dumb cluck! Did you really think of telling your Mama? In that case you might as well give up now . . . then you'll never find out if you've got second sight, believe me!'

Mardie did, she believed Abe! Because it was quite true, Mama liked Mardie to sleep at night, second sight or no. Then Abe reminded her of all the times she had climbed out over the verandah roof. It had been by day of course, but what you can do by day

84

you can do by night as well . . . unless you're a coward, of course!

'Well, coming or not?' asked Abe sternly.

Mardie didn't know where to put herself.

'I shall never keep awake till midnight, it won't *work.*'

But Abe was not going to let her off so lightly. He thought for a bit and then he said ·

'I think I might be able to persuade great-great-grandfather to come a little earlier for once, can you guess how?'

Mardie couldn't guess, because she was not as cunning as Abe.

'I'll put my alarm clock in the wash-house, but I'll set it three hours fast, what do you say to that? Then great-great-grandfather will think it's twelve o'clock when it's only nine, ha ha!'

'Ha ha,' said Mardie, but she didn't sound really happy.

'Well, coming?' said Abe, more sternly than before.

'Ye-e-s,' said Mardie, 'I'll do it.'

'Marvellous,' said Abe, 'one can rely on you.'

Mardie and Lisbet went to bed at seven every evening. Then Mama would come up and sit with them for a little while, telling stories and singing to them. Finally they all sang a song together, Mama and Mardie and Lisbet. Sometimes Papa was there too and they would sing two parts. '*Abide with me, Fast falls the eventide,*' they sang. Mardie always felt very happy because it sounded so beautiful, and even happier about the words themselves, although she didn't know why. Perhaps Lisbet was happy about the words

85

too. At least she didn't say what she used to say when she was little and had to learn them:

'This is boring, Mama. Let's do *Gentle Jesus* instead!'

But she had been only three then. Nowadays she knew the whole song and sang as hard as she could. 'Abide with me, Fast falls the eventide'. She sang 'soft', though, instead of 'fast'. Oh, how right she was, thought Mardie. Soft was just what the eventide was, when you were lying in your lovely soft bed and Mama tucked you in and the birches outside the window rustled so sweetly.

But that particular evening, eventide did not fall softly at all. That evening felt quite different. Mardie shuddered when she thought of what she was going to do, but it was the kind of shudder she didn't mind. There was something inside her which always drove her on to adventures. She liked excitement and she had made up her mind that she was going to the Nilssons' wash-house to find out if she had second sight. It was rather like going to the dentist – it was worse before it had been decided that she must go. After that it was not too bad. And if Abe could stand seeing ghosts, so could Mardie. At least, so she thought as long as she was lying here in her bed.

Mama and Papa had said goodnight long ago. Now Mardie was just lying waiting for Lisbet to fall asleep, because this was so secret that not even Lisbet was allowed to know.

'Are you asleep?' asked Mardie.

'Of course I'm not,' said Lisbet. 'Are you?'

'Oh, you are silly,' said Mardie.

She lay quiet for a bit, then tried again.

'Lisbet, are you asleep?'

'Not particularly,' said Lisbet, 'are you?'

'Oh, what a child,' Mardie was almost angry.

'Are you planning to stay awake all night?'

'Defuntly,' said Lisbet.

But the next minute she rolled over on her tummy and fell asleep.

Mardie had never dressed herself in the dark before. She did not dare light the oil-lamp because Lisbet might wake up or Mama might see a strip of light under the nursery door. But luckily that evening Mardie had laid out her clothes very tidily on a chair beside the bed and she soon had her vest and bodice

and knickers on. Then came an anxious moment . . .
suddenly there was only one stocking. She searched
wildly for the other. It really wouldn't look right to
come down to meet Abe's great-great-grandfather,
Lord as he was, with one bare leg. But at last she
found her stocking under the chair and her boots were
there too. It wasn't very easy to lace them in the dark
but she knotted them up as best she could. Then there
was just her dress and the big wool jersey which she
wore when she went out to play.

Mardie clenched her teeth . . . this was the most
difficult part. She had to open the nursery door and
creep right across the landing to the little window
over the verandah roof, and she had to do it so
quietly that Mama and Papa would not notice. They
were down in the living-room and when Mardie
opened the nursery door a crack she could hear their
talk like a muffled humming.

She got safely across the landing without anything
happening. She got the window open too, but it
gave the most ghastly screech just as she pushed it
open. There was a sudden silence in the living-room
and Mardie stood there nervously waiting to see what
would happen.

What happened was simply that Mama sat down
at the piano and began to play. She played a calm, safe
little tune. Mardie could hear the soft notes behind
her as she crawled across the verandah roof, and a
sinking feeling came over her. Everything that was
safe and peaceful she was leaving behind. In front of
her were nothing but darkness and danger.

It was November now. A dark, cold November
evening, and chillier than Mardie had thought it

would be. The wind was blowing through the trees. They had no leaves left to make a friendly rustling, they only rattled their branches, as if to scare people away. Mardie stood in the darkness outside Abe's window. She could see them in the kitchen, Abe and his mother and father, and she would very much have liked to join them in the light and warmth, but Abe had said she should stay outside the window and make a noise like an owl. Mardie obediently did as she had been told. It sounded so dreadful that she frightened herself and inside the kitchen Mrs Nilsson jumped. Abe also sprang to life. He leapt up from his chair and pulled on his cap. Now he was at the door, Mardie could see him in the misty light of the oil-lamp. For a nobleman, he was not particularly elegant. The knees of his trousers were patched and his pullover hung round him like a sack. He was extraordinarily spindly, too. Mardie had an idea that noblemen were generally fatter and perhaps a little better groomed, but she didn't know any besides Abe, so she couldn't be sure. Abe's hair was like a thicket and stuck out in tufts under his cap, but he was grinning delightedly and no doubt believed he looked like a nobleman.

He found Mardie in the darkness among the apple trees and came towards her eagerly.

'Now for it,' he said. 'Now for it, if we've managed to make great-great-grandfather think it's twelve o'clock.'

'Yes, now for it,' said Mardie with a shudder. 'Have you put the alarm clock in there?'

'You'd better believe it! And I've set the alarm too, so that the old man won't over-sleep. After all, he's not used to waking up at this hour.'

The wash-house lay right at the bottom of the Nilssons' garden, down by the stream. There was a little well-trodden pathway leading to it. Abe had a torch to light their way so that Mardie wouldn't go and hit her head on some mossy old apple tree – Abe was so kind and thoughtful!

'Can I hold your hand?' said Mardie. 'I can see better that way.'

'Can you?' said Abe. 'That's odd.'

He took Mardie's hand, which was cold and shaking a little.

'But when great-great-grandfather comes I'll leave go of you,' said Abe. 'He doesn't think it's proper for me to be mixing with people who haven't any noble blood in them.'

There stood the wash-house, dark and gloomy; it

certainly did look rather like a haunted house. And it was horribly silent. Could this really be the same house which was so full of cheerful sounds when Mrs Nilsson was doing the washing in there? There was the splash and thud of the wet clothes as she flung them into the big boiler and thumped and banged with the clothes beater, and the whole building was so full of steam that Mardie and Lisbet could scarcely see each other as they zigzagged among the piles of washing. It was fun to be in the wash-house then, and most fun of all in the loft. You could jump and shout and leap about as much as you liked and play hide-and-seek and tag. Under the roof beams there were owls, which didn't like it when Mardie and Lisbet jumped and shouted. They flew out through the skylights and did not come back until Mardie and Lisbet had gone. Perhaps the ghost did the same? Perhaps Lord Crow also flew out of the skylight whenever Mardie and Lisbet made a row up there. But just now he would be sitting in the darkness, huddled among the owls . . . huddled and waiting. Mardie clutched Abe, she was frightened and he could feel it. He had switched off the torch and was standing with his hand on the heavy key, about to turn it, but he hesitated.

'Tell me what you want to do,' he whispered. 'I thought you might enjoy seeing a ghost, but you can get out of it if you like.'

Just then they heard the alarm clock ringing in the wash-house, as if to wake up all the spirits of the night and tell them that Mardie had come. It sounded awful.

'Go if you like,' said Abe. 'You'll be in time, because it will be some time before great-great-grandfather shows a leg.'

91

Of course Mardie was so frightened that she was trembling, but how was she ever to find out if she had second sight if she didn't take her chance now?

'I do want to see him,' she muttered. 'But only a bit.'

'Right, then,' said Abe. 'But don't blame me if you pass out!'

He turned the key and opened the door softly.

It creaked horribly . . . if Lord Crow had not heard the alarm clock, which seemed unlikely, he would certainly wake up now.

Mardie stared into the great, black darkness and kept a firm hold of Abe's pullover. Without him she was lost, she knew, and she pleaded anxiously:

'Put on the torch so that we can see.'

But Abe did not put on the torch.

'You're not used to ghosts, I can see that. There's nothing that annoys them more than lighting them up with a torch. They get so angry, they snarl – have you ever heard a ghost snarl?'

Luckily for her, Mardie never had.

'You should be glad of that,' said Abe. 'I know someone who did, and he's still shivering.'

Mardie realized what madness it would be to light up Lord Crow with the torch so that he began to snarl. Abe knew best, and she followed him into the pitch darkness without any more protest. Abe shut the door behind them and it was as black as a sack. Somewhere in the middle of it Lord Crow would be lurking, quite creepy enough, even without the snarling. Mardie pressed nervously against Abe. They had stopped by the door and they stood there for some time in silence, waiting.

Then Mardie felt Abe start and heard him begin to pant.

'There! Now he's coming! There! By the boiler wall.'

Mardie screamed and clutched at Abe. She pressed herself against him and shut her eyes.

'Can you see him?' whispered Abe.

Mardie opened her eyes reluctantly and stared towards the boiler wall. She could see nothing but the great black darkness. Abe must be right. She had no more second sight than a pig, and just now she was glad of it.

'Can't you really see him?' whispered Abe. 'Can't you see a white monster there, glowing with light?'

'Nooo,' said Mardie truthfully.

'That's odd,' said Abe. Abe himself could see him quite clearly, and talk to him as well.

'Noble lord, where have you hidden the treasure? Give me an answer, if you think you would like to,'

But there was no answer. The lord obviously did not think he would like to.

'Stubborn as usual,' Abe whispered to Mardie. Then he said loudly:

'I am noble myself and I need the treasure . . . be kind, great-great-grandfather, we're related, after all!'

Then he whispered again to Mardie:

'He looks gruesome . . . can't you really see him?'

'Nooo,' Mardie assured him, 'I can't have second sight.'

'Don't let that worry you,' said Abe. 'Sometimes it takes quite a long time before you sort of get going and then suddenly you can see ghosts wherever you turn.'

But Mardie was certain that she did not have second

93

sight, she had tested it now and all she wanted was to get away.

Then Abe started once again, and whispered to Mardie:

'Look, he's beckoning me, he wants me to come . . . Yes, great-great-grandfather,' he said aloud, 'I'm coming.'

But Mardie clung tightly to him.

'No, don't go,' she whispered in horror.

'I must,' whispered Abe, 'he's going to show me the treasure. You stay here.'

Suddenly Mardie was alone in the darkness. She could hear Abe tiptoeing across the floor and she did not know what to do with herself. She dared not follow him and she dared not stay where she was.

'Abe,' she called, 'Abe!'

But Abe did not answer. He had vanished in the darkness, and the seconds passed. Abe did not return. They were long seconds for Mardie.

'Abe,' she called again. 'Abe, I want to go home!'

But at that moment she *saw*! Oh, horrors, she *saw*, she had second sight . . . she actually saw the white monster glowing with light. He was standing over by the boiler wall, Lord Crow, as sure as fate!

Mardie screamed as she had never screamed before. She screamed and screamed and fumbled for the door to get out. The light round Lord Crow had already gone out. She could no longer see him, but Mardie went on screaming. From the darkness she could hear Abe's voice.

'Quiet, Mardie, don't scream in that awful way, you'll go and scare Lord Crow away, if you do that!'

But Mardie wasn't listening, she was frantic. All she

94

wanted was to get out . . . out!

Alma had had the evening off and gone into town. She had just come home and was putting the key in the kitchen door when Mardie came rushing up. Without a word she flung her arms round Alma and buried her face in her tummy, so violently that Alma nearly fell over.

'What in heaven's name are you doing out at this hour?' said Alma.

Mardie just went on whimpering and Alma could feel her body shaking all over. She asked no more questions but pushed Mardie quickly into the kitchen and lighted the lamp. This was not easily done because Mardie clung to her all the time as if she were being drowned at sea.

'What in heaven's name has happened?' said Alma.

She took Mardie to the kitchen sofa, pulled her on to her lap and rocked her.

'Alma, I've seen a ghost,' whispered Mardie. 'Oh Alma, I've got second sight!'

It was some time before Alma could get anything more out of her. She could scarcely speak and after all, Abe had told her she was not to speak of it to a living soul. But whatever happened, she had to talk it out of herself and so at last Alma heard the whole story of Lord Crow in the Nilssons' wash-house.

Alma blazed with anger.

'I'm going to go and pull that Abe's hair out, I'll give him ghosts!'

But Mardie defended him. 'He can't help having second sight.'

'Can't he,' said Alma furiously. 'Just you wait until

I've finished with him! He won't have second sight any more, I promise you. The Right Honourable Lord Abe can go to blazes!'

Luckily Mama and Papa were asleep and Alma promised Mardie not to tell them.

'Yes, because if Madam heard about this,' said Alma, 'you'd have put your foot inside the Nilssons' house for the last time. But I'm going to say something to Abe that he won't forget.'

Next day when Mardie came home from school, Abe was hanging over the fence as if he'd been waiting for someone. His hair was still in place, so Alma had not pulled it out, but he must have been hearing a few home-truths, because he was looking a little ashamed of himself. He whistled to Mardie and she came obediently.

'I didn't really believe you had second sight all that much,' he said. 'If I had, I'd never have taken you to the wash-house.'

Mardie trembled as soon as he mentioned the wash-house.

'I shall never go there again.'

'Why on earth not?' said Abe. 'There's no need to be frightened of great-great-grandfather, he won't be coming back.'

'How do you know?' asked Mardie, surprised.

'He's finished haunting it now, you see. Because I've dug up the treasure now, you see.'

'Have you?' asked Mardie.

'Yes, but it's a secret. So don't you go telling that Alma about it.'

Mardie promised, shamefaced. Then she looked wide-eyed at Abe.

'Are you rich now, Abe?'

Abe spat thoughtfully on the ground.

'Humph! I must say I think great-great-grand-father was making too much fuss about a mere 25 pence!'

He put his hand in his trouser pocket and pulled out two tens and a five.

'Is that all there was?' asked Mardie.

'Yes, that's all. But remember, great-great-grand-father lived over a hundred years ago. In those days 25 pence was no small potatoes, so perhaps we shouldn't be surprised that he haunted the place.'

Abe pushed 10 pence into Mardie's hand.

'This is for you. For your toil and sweat, or whatever it's called.'

Mardie's face lit up. How kind Abe was!

'Thank you very much, Abe.'

'Don't mention it,' said Abe. 'It's ghost money of course, but it buys just as much as ordinary money.'

Then the Right Honourable Lord Abe disappeared into his kitchen, leaving Mardie staring delightedly at the ghost money.

To think that it had been lying in the Nilssons' wash-house for over a hundred years, and yet it was so bright and looked so real. It would certainly be all right for buying a paper doll. And there was the king's picture on it. Yes, it looked just as a coin should look!

7

The snows and the storms are on their way . . .

Now the great winter darkness lay over Junedale. It would soon be Christmas. Mardie and Lisbet talked about it every night.

'What a good thing there is such a thing as Christmas,' said Mardie. 'I think it's the best thing they've ever thought of.'

'Defuntly,' said Lisbet.

And they rattled their piggy-banks and listened to all the money there was inside. That rattle was going to turn into Christmas presents and that was why it was such a beautiful rattle.

They had a calendar on the wall in the nursery. Every morning they pulled off one sheet and knew they were one day closer to Christmas.

You could feel that Christmas was coming at school, too. Teacher read Christmas stories and the children had to learn their carols. Mardie came home and sang them to Lisbet!

> '*The snows and the storms are on their way*
> *Through the valleys and hills in the north,*'

she sang.

And in no time at all Mardie's Christmas holidays
began. 'Oh, why do we have to have holidays!' That

was what she had said on that first day of school so long ago. But now she had been a schoolgirl for a whole term and she thought that Christmas holidays were almost as good an idea as Christmas itself.

Alma and Ida had already begun on the great Christmas cleaning. They had taken down all the curtains and there were scouring pails in the most unlikely places. Alma went about with a long panel brush, dusting the walls and the ceiling. Mardie and Lisbet climbed over the scouring buckets and were always in the way and all the time they teased Alma:

> '*Alma the round is on her way*
> *Over ceilings and floors in the north.*'

they sang to her. Every time, Lisbet giggled so much that she almost sat down in the scouring pails.

'You do think of good rhymes, Mardie!'

But Alma chased them with the panel brush and sang:

> '*Now this little brush is on its way*
> *And we're soon going to spank somebody in the north!*'

But she was not angry. Alma was never angry with Mardie and Lisbet.

Mama prepared sausages and salt bacon and brewed juniper wine and dipped candles. Mardie and Lisbet were allowed to help with all kinds of things. They baked gingerbread and boiled up toffee and made little marzipan pigs and cut out tissue paper for the Christmas decoration round the kitchen range. Every day unusual things happened and it felt more and more like Christmas. Over Junedale lay the most

100

wonderful fragrance of gingerbread and toffee and cakes. Mardie sniffed the scent up her nostrils and closed her eyes.

'Christmas . . . it's already smelling of Christmas!'

In the evening they wrote long lists of the presents they wanted from Father Christmas.

'Robinson Crusoe, lots of paper dolls, toy soldiers, skis, a pink rose for my hair,' was what Mardie had on her list. She read it out to Lisbet.

'You're potty, Mardie,' said Lisbet. 'Do you really want a rose?'

'Not at all,' said Mardie. 'I just wrote it because it sounds so beautiful.'

They wondered a lot about what to give Mama and Papa for Christmas. Mardie asked Mama, while they were boiling up the toffee:

'Mama, what would you like best of all?'

'Two really good, sweet girls,' said Mama.

Mardie's eyes turned shiny and her voice trembled a little.

'But what would you do with Lisbet and me?'

Mama stroked her hair and explained that she didn't want any *other* little girls, she just wanted Mardie and Lisbet to go on being as good and sweet as ever.

Lisbet, however, thought it would not be a bad idea to have two new little girls in the house.

'We could play with them,' she said. 'But they wouldn't be allowed to live in the nursery, sucks to them, because that's where Mardie and I live.'

It was beginning to be cold. Alma lit a big fire in the nursery every morning, rattling and clattering the stove doors until Mardie and Lisbet woke up. Then they would lie in their beds watching the flames through the little panes in the doors and listening to the fire crackling behind them. It was such a lovely sound to wake up to.

One morning they woke up early. They thought it was an ordinary day, but it wasn't at all. It was the last Sunday in Advent, four candles were burning in the Advent candle-holder on the desk and Alma, who had just lit the fire, was standing by Mardie's bed, looking mysterious.

'Something marvellous happened last night,' she said, 'can you guess what?'

'A ghost,' Mardie suggested.

After her evening in the Nilssons' wash-house she thought ghosts were what happened in the night.

'There aren't any ghosts, silly,' said Alma. 'That was only Abe, playing the fool with a sheet and a torch, I told you that.'

Alma had tried to convince Mardie of this many

times but Mardie did not believe her. Abe could not be so treacherous – anyone else, but not Abe!

'Guess something else,' said Alma. 'Something nice has happened.'

'Ghosts are nice,' said Lisbet.

'I don't think so,' said Alma. 'Now guess!'

'Has it been snowing?' asked Mardie excitedly.

'No,' said Alma, 'but there's ice on the stream.'

Mardie and Lisbet shrieked and jumped up out of their beds. The room was not warm yet, but they didn't worry about that, they were in a hurry. They got dressed, pulling on their woolly leggings and thick jerseys and caps and mittens and then they were outside.

'Just for a little while,' Alma shouted after them, 'you must come in and have breakfast soon.'

'Yes, yes,' said Mardie and Lisbet.

The birches round Junedale were chalk-white with frost and in the sky over the woodshed roof the sun shone bright red.

'I love this kind of weather,' said Mardie.

Actually she loved all kinds of weather. Mostly the weather was the kind she didn't notice, it was just there. But this was the kind of weather she noticed. It was beautiful, rather in the way that tunes and words can be beautiful, Mardie thought, they make you nicer.

Mardie and Lisbet ran down to the stream. The frosty, frozen grass crunched under their feet.

'Perhaps I shall give you *two* Christmas presents, Lisbet,' said Mardie as she ran.

'You're potty, Mardie,' said Lisbet.

Of course it would be nice to get two Christmas

presents, but just now she was only thinking about the ice.

It's a wonderful moment when you put your foot on the smooth, dark ice and see whether it's holding. Oh, it was holding so well that at the first step Mardie felt herself sliding almost all the way across the stream.

It was not quiet true that all that ice had arrived overnight. It has been freezing for a whole week, but Mardie and Lisbet had not noticed that the stream had grown stiller day by day. Only Alma had noticed and this morning before anyone else was awake she had gone down to test the ice with a thick pole. No one need be afraid to walk on it.

'Because if it holds Alma, it'll hold us,' said Mardie.

'Defuntly,' said Lisbet.

Mardie and Lisbet slid to their hearts' content. Their cheeks grew red and their breath puffed out of their mouths like white smoke. They could not understand how people could go on sleeping when there was something so delightful to do. But over at *Repose* no one seemed to be awake. Abe simply didn't know! He didn't know that the stream was like one smooth, shining path to slide along. It wound its way along in bends and bays and round every bend there were more splendid ice slides lying in wait. If you went on past *Repose* and kept going long enough you came to Appletree Lake, which really was right out in the country, and there was a farm there called Appletree Hill.

'I wonder if we could go and pay a visit to the Peter Carlssons at Appletree Hill?' suggested Mardie.

'Would Mama let us?' asked Lisbet.

Mama was still asleep because it was Sunday. They

couldn't wake her up to ask about such a little thing.

'Of course she would,' said Mardie. 'Not if we were going by road, of course, it would take much too long, but if we slide we'll be there in a moment.'

'Right then,' said Lisbet.

Neither of them remembered what Alma had said about breakfast. With happy hearts they slid away in the direction of Appletree Hill.

'Ice is one of the things I love,' said Mardie.

'Ice is one of the things everyone loves,' said Lisbet.

But Mardie didn't simply love it . . . she was so happy that her heart was almost bursting from her breast. This ice path was a miracle. The winter stream and the summer stream were so different. They used to row there with Papa on summer evenings, sometimes all the way to Appletree Hill to buy eggs. Then it was a gentle, kindly little stream, rippling along among green trees. Soft, green branches hung out over the water so that Mardie and Lisbet could pull off leaves as they sat in the boat – yes, the summer stream was gentle and kindly. But the winter stream seemed to be enchanted. The dark, shining ice and the silent trees covered with frost reflecting the sun, red and strange, were beautiful in a frosty, cold, fantastic way which made Mardie wild with joy. Faster and faster she slid, growing wilder and wilder, feeling almost as if she were flying. Lisbet was left far behind.

'Wait for me!' she shouted.

She was growing tired after sliding, she wanted to walk, and not too fast, either. Mardie would have to wait until Lisbet caught up with her.

'How far is it to Appletree Hill?' asked Lisbet suspiciously.

'Not far at all,' Mardie assured her. 'We'll be there soon.'

'Hold my hand,' said Lisbet, putting her fist in Mardie's. So they trudged on, hand in hand, very slowly now. At every fresh bend they expected to see the lake and Appletree Hill, but every time it was just the same old stream ahead of them. Lisbet began to be tired of it.

'Do you know what, Mardie,' she said, 'I'm hungry.'

It was then that they remembered what Alma had said. 'You must come in soon and have your breakfast,' she'd said. And here they were, a long way from home, gazing anxiously at one another.

Mardie was hungry too, but she wouldn't turn back. It could only be a very, very short way to Appletree Hill now and it would be nice to rest there a while.

'We can buy an egg each from Mrs Carlsson,' she said. 'And when we've bought it we'll ask them to let us cook it and eat it up at once.'

'Have we any money?' asked Lisbet.

'No, that's just it,' said Mardie thoughtfully. But then she remembered something. She *was* wearing her check shirt, and if she remembered rightly, there would be a two pence piece in her pocket.

'I know I've got two pence because I put it there yesterday,' she said, beginning to dig into her pocket.

'Can you get two eggs for two pence?' asked Lisbet.

Mardie shook her head.

'Not really. But we can try. We'll say we want eggs for two pence and see what happens.' But the tiresome thing was that there was no two pence piece in her pocket. It had gone.

'So what shall we do?' asked Lisbet.

Mardie shrugged her shoulders.

'Oh well, two pence more or less isn't all that important when you're buying eggs.'

Lisbet didn't think so either.

'We'll go there all the same,' said Mardie. 'Mrs Carlsson may invite us to breakfast, and we must say yes *immediately*!'

The thought that breakfast might be waiting for them around the next corner refreshed them. They started sliding again. They slid for some time and then they walked a long way further, but still there was no sign of Appletree Hill.

'Perhaps they put the whole farm somewhere else in winter,' suggested Lisbet.

'Don't be childish,' said Mardie, but she was beginning to wonder too.

'This is very strange,' she said. 'If we don't see Appletree Hill when we get round that corner we must be under a spell, and that'll be our bad luck.'

The idea began to nag at Mardie. It was all witch's work. The trees, so beautiful and dead in their wonderful, white-frosted branches . . . trees like that could only grow in enchanted woods. The dark, smooth ice which sent children crazy and enticed them away, was a witch's pathway which had no end. Horrible little winter witches slid up and down there at night when it was too cold to fly on their broomsticks. Yes, the whole thing was witch's work.

But Lisbet did not want be under a spell, she said so determinedly, with a great many sobs and tears.

And just think . . . as they swung round the bend, what should they see but Appletree Farm, with its barn and its stables and its red farmhouse!

Lisbet stopped crying at once.

'Appletree Hill is a nice farm,' she said happily.

Mardie thought so too.

'I hope they're in,' she said. 'Especially Tom and Marie.'

Tom and Marie were the Appletree Hill children and Mardie liked them, although they were terribly old, almost twenty. They could not have come at a better moment. At Appletree Hill everyone was just sitting down to breakfast; Peter Carlsson and Mrs Carlsson and Tom and Marie, when Mardie and Lisbet came in through the door like two red-cheeked Christmas angels.

'Have you got any eggs?' asked Lisbet, before anyone else could get a word out.

Mardie pinched her. Silly Lisbet, that was all wrong! It would have been the right way to start if they had had that two pence piece, but they hadn't.

'My dear children, have you come all this way in the cold to buy eggs?' asked Mrs Carlsson. 'How many eggs would your mother like?'

Mardie and Lisbet felt embarrassed. They didn't know how to explain that Mama had not sent them at all. Mardie was getting more and more annoyed with Lisbet. She was the one who had spoiled it all. You don't invite egg-buyers to breakfast, you only do that to people who have come to say hello.

'Actually, we're just out for a walk,' said Mardie.

'Yes, because we haven't any money,' said Lisbet. 'We're out for a walk without money.'

'I see, so that's how it is,' said Peter Carlsson, dunking his roll in the coffee. 'Yes, it's fine weather for walking . . . with no money!'

109

'Very fine,' said Mardie. 'It gives you such an appetite.'

'I can well imagine it,' said Peter Carlsson.

But he didn't seem able to imagine anything much. Mrs Carlsson was more intelligent.

'Perhaps you'd like some porridge?' she asked.

'Yes please,' said Mardie and Lisbet at once.

They had their caps and jerseys and mittens off in a flash and before Marie even had time to get out their dishes, they were sitting at the table.

The Carlssons had finished breakfast but they all stayed at the table just to talk to Lisbet and Mardie.

'So you were just out for a walk, so to speak,' said Peter Carlsson, laughing gently.

Mardie's and Lisbet's mouth were so full of porridge that they could not answer, they simply nodded. Mrs Carlsson gave them big rye-bread sandwiches. They ate their sandwiches and shovelled porridge into themselves – you really could see what good weather it was for producing an appetite.

'Porridge is almost my favourite thing,' said Mardie. 'Don't you think so, Lisbet?'

'No,' said Lisbet, briefly but firmly. Of course she liked porridge, especially now, but it wasn't her favourite thing, and Lisbet always said exactly what she thought.

The Carlssons laughed at her. They had a special laugh here at Appletree Hill; they all laughed in the same way, a quiet, kind sort of laugh.

'Well, what is your favourite thing?' asked Mrs Carlsson.

Lisbet considered.

'Gooseberry cream . . . and cream . . . and more

110

cream.'

The Carlssons laughed again.

'Gooseberry cream and cream and more cream,' said Peter Carlsson, 'that's a terrible lot of cream!'

Mardie explained. She was the only one who understood what Lisbet meant.

'Gooseberry cream is gooseberry cream and cream is apple cream and more cream is all the other kinds of cream.'

Tom laughed as well.

'Gooseberry cream and cream and more cream! Don't you live on anything but cream at Junedale?'

'Of course we do,' said Lisbet indignantly. 'We live on ice-cream too . . . when I was five I had as much ice as I liked, at least five kilos!'

'Well, bless my soul,' said Mrs Carlsson, 'are you five already? When was that then?'

'Oh, she doesn't know,' said Mardie.

Lisbet glared at her.

'I don't know? Yes I *do* know!'

'Do you? When was it then?'

'On my birthday . . . so there,' said Lisbet, sticking out her tongue at Mardie. So Mardie stuck out her tongue right back at Lisbet. Then they remembered that you don't do that kind of thing when you're out. Instead they said thank you very politely for their meal, going round the table and shaking hands and bobbing to each one in turn – Peter Carlsson and Mrs Carlsson and Tom and Marie.

They were full now, but a bit tired as well. It was nice sitting here in the kitchen and they really had no desire to go out into the cold again and walk home.

'I think I'm going to give your Papa a ring,' said

111

Peter Carlsson. 'They may not know at home that you're here to buy eggs . . . without any money.'

Then Mardie and Lisbet began to be ashamed and they felt very anxious when Peter Carlsson rang up Junedale. Mardie stood beside him, tugging at his sleeve.

'Ask if we could stay here and rest for a bit.'

Peter Carlsson did: he asked if Mardie and Lisbet could stay at Appletree Hill.

'I can drive them back in a little while,' he said. Mardie and Lisbet looked at each other, grinning.

But then Peter Carlsson handed the receiver to Mardie.

'Your Papa would like to talk to you,' he said, and Mardie stopped grinning.

'Listen, Miss Marvellous,' said Papa. 'How would it be if you were to think for once in your life . . . going off all that way in this cold, what if you had frozen your noses off, what would you have said to that?'

Mardie thought about it afterwards. Could you really freeze your nose off, how dreadful! There you were, walking along quite peacefully with Lisbet, and suddenly your noses would fall off and lie on the ice like two cold little blobs of skin and bone . . . Yes, what would you say to that? 'Goodbye,' perhaps . . . Mardie shuddered to think of it. She was all ready to start crying over her lost nose, when she suddenly remembered that both she and Lisbet still had their noses, what luck!

Lisbet was using hers just then. She snuggled it into Tom's thick coat which was hanging over the arm of a chair.

'It does smell good,' she said. 'It smells of the cow

byre, could we go there?'

Tom was just as kind and cooperative as his father.

'Yes, of course we can,' he said, laughing in that quiet, jolly way, as if he knew something funny that no one else knew about.

So he took them over to the cow byre and showed them the big bull and all the cows and calves. In a pen lay an almost new-born calf and they liked that best of all. He could only just clamber onto his legs, but he managed to get over to the door and poke his damp nose up at Mardie and Lisbet. They gave him their fingers to lick and Lisbet told him it would soon be Christmas, in case he didn't know.

Then they went with Tom to the stables. There were

113

four horses there, Titus and Mona and Freya and
Conker. When Mardie and Lisbet last saw them it was
summertime and they were out in the fields. Now they
were standing in their loose-boxes. They whinnied a
little when Mardie and Lisbet came in. Conker was the
nicest and the ugliest, he was such a strange, yellowish
colour.

'It doesn't matter how you look as long as you're
nice,' said Mardie.

They went into his loose-box and patted him and brushed him with a horse brush and gave him hay and oats. Tom looked on, laughing gently to himself.

'Which was the manger that little Jesus lay in!' asked Lisbet suddenly. She thought there was only one stable in the world and that was here, at Appletree Hill.

Mardie explained to her that that was in quite a different stable, far away in the country of the Jews.

'How do you know?' asked Lisbet.

'I know it's true because Teacher told us.'

Lisbet was not at all satisfied.

'No it wasn't, He was lying in Conker's manger, that's what they said at my school. And Conker was very nice and didn't bite Him, he just nuzzled Him to see who it was.'

Mardie looked round the dim stable. In fact, she too would have liked Jesus' manger to be here, at Appletree Hill.

'Perhaps it was here after all,' she said enthusiastically. 'And Mary put candles in all the windows and Peter Carlsson and Mrs Carlsson sat in the kitchen and saw the light and Mrs Carlsson said: "Who in the world is in the stable tonight?"'

Lisbet knew the answer to that.

'It's only the Baby Jesus,' she said. 'He's lying in Conker's crib and Conker's nuzzling Him and that makes Jesus laugh because He likes it.'

'Aren't I sitting in the kitchen too, seeing the light from the stable?' asked Tom.

'Now you're being really silly, Tom,' said Mardie. 'That happened ages ago and you weren't even born then.'

While they were in the stable the weather had changed. The red sun had gone and now the sky was an even grey and there was the smell of snow in the air.

'Hurrah, it's going to snow,' said Mardie.

And it did, it snowed a great deal, it came tumbling down all over Appletree Hill.

'I can't drive you home in this weather,' said Peter Carlsson. 'We'd better wait until the snow is over.'

'Yes, we'd better,' said Mardie and Lisbet.

They had nothing at all against waiting until the snow was over. Marie had kept the dolls she had had when she was little and she brought them out for Mardie and Lisbet to play with. They lined them up on the kitchen sofa and changed their clothes and had great fun. All the time it went on snowing.

'I think this is going to be a sleigh drive,' said Peter Carlsson. 'But in any case we'll wait until the snow is over.'

'Yes, we will,' said Mardie and Lisbet. They went on playing with the dolls, having a wonderful time on Appletree Hill. Then Mrs Carlsson was beckoning Lisbet.

'Now, which is your most favourite of all, gooseberry cream or cream or the other cream?'

'Gooseberry cream,' said Lisbet.

'Then it's lucky that's the very one we're going to have for pudding, and not cream or the other cream,' said Mrs Carlsson. 'Come on, it's lunch time!'

So Mardie and Lisbet had roast pork and onion sauce and gooseberry cream with milk at Appletree Hill. And all the time it went on snowing.

'This snow is never going to stop,' said Peter Carlsson. 'Perhaps we'd better be going all the same,

otherwise they'll be thinking in Junedale that we've kidnapped you.'

'It may stop soon, ' said Mrs Carlsson.

But it didn't. More and more snow fell on Appletree Hill. The fence posts already had tall white hats on and the flakes filled the air so thickly that you could scarcely see the barn from the kitchen window. Soon dusk began to fall and Peter Carlsson said:

'Now, Tom, you'd better hitch up the snow plough, otherwise I shall never get to Junedale with these two.'

So Tom went out and hitched Mona and Freya to the snow plough and Peter Carlsson hitched Titus and Conker to the basket sleigh and Mardie and Lisbet were tucked into it under a fur rug so that only their noses stuck out. They couldn't even wave goodbye to Mrs Carlsson and Marie, who were standing in the window watching as they left. Peter Carlsson sat on the driver's seat and drove the sleigh and Tom drove the snow plough in front of them.

'It takes four horses to get us home from Appletree Hill, that's a lot,' said Mardie.

'Four horses and a snow plough,' said Lisbet, 'that's almost like a whole sleigh-ride party.'

So they played they were on a sleigh-ride party. They burrowed under the fur and listened to the sound of bells, four bells ringing for Mardie and Lisbet as they came driving home to Junedale.

'It was a good thing we went to Appletree Hill after all,' said Mardie.

'All the same, this snow is going on for ever,' said Peter Carlsson.

Perhaps it wasn't as nice for him on the driver's seat

as it was for Mardie and Lisbet under their fur.

'We could sing, to cheer him up a bit,' Mardie whispered to Lisbet.

Lisbet agreed:

> '*The snows and the storms are on their way*
> *over valleys and hills in the north,*'

they sang.

> '*Oh, Christmas time,*' sang Mardie.
> '*Oh, childhood's time,*' sang Lisbet,
> '*Oh, childhood's time in the no-o-orth.*'

But by then they were already at Junedale's gate.

'Look, there are four candles in the window,' said Lisbet.

'Yes, because it's Advent, you see,' said Mardie.

8

Christmas at Junedale

'There we are, then,' said Alma, the night before Christmas Eve. 'Now it's ready! Oof, I'm tired, but everything is ready!'

'Apart from the Christmas tree,' said Lisbet. 'Papa and Mama are going to decorate it tonight while we're asleep.'

Mardie said nothing. She just snuggled up and shivered, in the way she did when everything was so wonderful she could scarcely bear it.

Yes, Christmas could come to Junedale now, everything was ready to receive it. Every nook and cranny was scrubbed and clean; all the windows had white, freshly starched curtains, there were candles in all the candle-sticks and bright new mats in the kitchen, the copper pans were shining on the walls and the kitchen range was decorated with red and green tissue paper, as festive as Christmas itself.

The living-room was filled with the scent of white hyacinths which Mama had been growing just for Christmas, and the fir tree, standing there green and fresh, waiting to be decorated, was scented too.

'We've got so much food, I think it will last till next

Christmas,' said Alma. Mardie and Lisbet thought so
too, because they had been down to the cellar to
look. On the big gate-legged table down there the
Christmas ham crowded against the pork brawn and
the spare ribs against the liver sausage and herring
salad and meatballs; rows of smoked sausage and
minced sausage hung from the ceiling; there was
juniper juice in its jar, pickled fish in its tub and curd

121

cake in its bowl. Everything was ready. The loaves and the rye bread and the saffron buns lay stacked in the bread chest, the gingerbread and macaroons, oatmeal biscuits and twists filled the cake tins – Christmas could come! The war which was going on somewhere out there in the world, and which Mardie told Lisbet about at night, was nowhere to be seen for the moment in Junedale; not even the sparrows need go hungry. In the evening Papa put the Christmas sheaves up in the apple trees so that the sparrows would also know when they woke up that it was Christmas-time.

Alma had stocked up with wood for all the Christmas fires and she had shovelled the snow to make funny little paths to the gate and the woodshed and the stream, yes, to the stream, because that was the path Father Christmas would take and it would be a pity if he couldn't get through all the snow, Mardie and Lisbet thought. But this year he would do very well, this year he would have no trouble, because the snow plough had been all the way along the stream. Tom had driven back that way to Appletree Hill on Sunday after ploughing for Mardie and Lisbet; Father Christmas would be glad when he came driving up in his sleigh tomorrow.

It was a good thing in many ways that Tom had ploughed along the stream. Abe had made an ice merry-go-round, which gave Mardie and Lisbet a lot of fun, especially when they sat in it and Abe pulled and they swung round so fast it made them dizzy.

But Abe could not often leave his stove: a great many buns were needed for Christmas. Mrs Nilsson went to the market to sell them every day. No one knew what Mr Nilsson did, but he was very busy, it seemed; at least he was seldom at home.

Then, the night before Christmas Eve, Mardie took a trip over to *Repose* to see what Abe was up to. And just imagine, Abe was scrubbing the kitchen floor! But he stopped at once when Mardie came in.

'I was just clearing up a bit,' he explained to her. But he had already scrubbed half the kitchen. You could clearly see where he had got to, the scrubbed part was not nearly so black as the unscrubbed. Mardie looked round . . . otherwise, there were no Christmas decorations to be seen in *Repose!* The curtains and the embroidered shelf edges had not been washed, everything was just as usual, and that was all wrong on the day before Christmas Eve, Mardie knew.

'Haven't you got everything ready yet?' she asked.

Abe looked surprised.

'What do you mean . . . ready?'

Mardie didn't quite know what to say.

'It . . . it's Christmas Eve tomorrow.'

'Of course we've got everything ready,' said Abe. 'Come and have a look!'

He went ahead of Mardie to the little room beside the kitchen and there was a paper hanging, covered with bearded Father Christmases, pinned on the wall.

'What do you say to that?' he said triumphantly. 'Ma and Pa haven't seen it yet, but their jaws are going to drop, mark my words!'

Mardie was still not satisfied.

'Haven't you got a Christmas tree?'

'While there's life there's hope,' said Abe. 'Pa may be bringing one when he comes home this evening. If he hasn't forgotten, that is. But if he has, I shall go out and get one in the woods tomorrow, because a Christ-

123

mas tree I will have!'

Mardie thought about their own Christmas tree at home in Junedale and one of those little shivers of excitement ran through her.

'Don't you think Christmas is wonderful, Abe?'

'Sure is,' said Abe. 'It's good to have everything nice. I like that hanging there,'

Mardie thought the hanging with the bearded Father Christmases on it was beautiful too, but it meant that there was only a Christmas decoration in that one little spot and Mardie wanted it to be Christmas everywhere. Abe was obviously not so fussy.

'Do you think you'll get a lot of Christmas presents?' asked Mardie.

'While there's life there's hope,' said Abe. 'I don't know if Pa and Ma will remember. But do you want to see what I've bought? Swear you won't tell a living soul!'

Mardie promised. Then Abe opened the wardrobe door cautiously. There stood a brand new oil-lamp with a white globe. It looked expensive and elegant.

'That's quite a different story from this old lamp we've got now,' said Abe.

'Is it a Christmas present?' asked Mardie.

'Oh well, Pa and Ma will get it and they can call it a Christmas present or whatever they like,' said Abe. 'It was as expensive as nobody's business, but I earned every penny of it myself.'

Mardie left rather thoughtfully. The oil-lamp and the bearded Father Christmases were certainly both very good, and yet they made her homesick for Junedale. At Abe's house you couldn't really believe it would be Christmas tomorrow and that made her

uneasy. She talked it over with Lisbet after they had gone to bed.

'How would it be if we were to wake up and it wasn't Christmas at all but just Friday, for instance?'

'I'd go and drown myself,' said Lisbet, because that was what Alma always said and Lisbet was quick to copy.

But Lisbet did not need to drown herself, because it was Christmas Eve when they woke up. It was still black outside the window but Papa was standing in the nursery door with a lighted candle and they heard Mama playing the piano downstairs. 'Christmas has come again,' she played.

'Yes, Christmas has come again,' said Papa. 'Happy Christmas, my sweethearts?'

'Happy Christmas, Papa!' shouted Mardie and Lisbet. And they jumped out of their beds and down the stairs into the living-room. There was the Christmas tree with its lighted candles, more beautiful than they remembered a tree could be, the log-fire was burning in the stove and the fir tree and the fire and the hyacinths gave off such a heavenly scent. There was no doubt that it was Christmas!

For a moment they were completely silenced. Then they came to life again and bounded across the floor, giddy with the joys of Christmas. They skipped and hopped and danced and sang and Sasso barked. There was no doubt that it was Christmas.

Then Alma came in with the Christmas coffee and they all sat in front of the fire drinking it, Mama and Papa and Alma and Mardie and Lisbet. For Mardie and Lisbet it was wonderful to be allowed to sit in front of the fire in their nightdresses drinking coffee.

'It's because it's Christmas,' said Mardie.

'Yes, it's because it's Christmas,' said Mama.

Mardie looked anxiously at her to see if she was tired. But Mama was simply happy, luckily, and not tired at all. *Everyone* had to be happy, *everyone* had to enjoy Christmas, otherwise something was wrong for Mardie. That was why she had begged Mama when she was toiling away at the Christmas cleaning:

'You *mustn't* be tired on Christmas Eve, promise!'

'No, how could I be tired on *Christmas Eve*?' said Mama.

And here she sat now, with Papa and Alma, and all three of them looked as if they were enjoying Christmas just as much as Mardie and Lisbet. Oh, how lovely it was!

Soon it grew light outside. The sparrows had woken up and were already sitting among the Christmas sheaves. Mardie and Lisbet looked at them through the dining-room window.

'Do the sparrows know it's Christmas, Papa?' asked Lisbet.

'They may not,' said Papa. 'But I think they understand the Christmas sheaves.'

'But I, I understand every . . . everything,' said Lisbet.

There was just one thing that neither Lisbet nor Mardie understood. Why was it that Christmas Eve, of all days, had to be twice as long as any other day? Who had thought that one up? Mama did what she could to make the weary hours pass a little faster. First she sent Mardie and Lisbet to Ida with the usual Christmas hamper. Ida must have Christmas ham and preserves and spare ribs, too, she must have sausage and liver sausage and bread and cakes and coffee and apples and candles. Mama packed them all together in the red basket and Mardie and Lisbet tramped off through the winter cold.

Ida was all by herself in her cottage, her daughters were far away in America. Mardie stood in her parlour worrying . . . perhaps Ida didn't think Christmas was fun at all? But there was no need for Mardie to worry. Ida sat in her wicker-chair in front of the open hearth with her feet in a basin of hot water, looking very pleased.

'I tell you, I tell you, me and my feet, we both know it's Christmas. Three long blessed days when we can keep quite still and do nothing.'

She was delighted with the Christmas basket and had to taste the liver sausage and the preserves right away and she patted the fat round smoked sausage happily.

'I ask you, is it right? Here you come, bringing me all the food you can bring, and here I am sitting like any countess, just splashing my feet about and stuffing myself, is it right?'

They couldn't stay long with Ida, because they had to go home and dip bread in the pot.

'Happy Christmas, Ida,' said Lisbet and Mardie as they went. And Ida sat there with her feet in the basin and a slice of preserve in her hand, looking as if she really was having a happy Christmas.

Outside in the yard Mia and Mattie were shovelling snow.

'Snotty noses are going to get what for!' said Mattie as soon as she saw Mardie and Lisbet, but Mia gave her a shove.

'Hold your tongue on Christmas Eve, at least!'

Mia smiled at Mardie and Lisbet, to show that she at least knew how to behave on Christmas Eve. She even said Happy Christmas to them.

'Happy Christmas,' said Mardie and Lisbet.

'Happy Christmas, snotty noses,' said Mattie. 'Mia and I have got new red drawers from the poor-box, sucks to you, you haven't!'

Then Mia shoved Mattie so that she fell over backwards in the snow and screamed:

'Can't you hold your tongue on Christmas Eve, at least!'

Mardie and Lisbet went away and they could hear Mattie howling a long way up the road.

Christmas Eve crawled on bit by bit. Mardie and Lisbet did their dipping in the pot thoroughly, not because they particularly liked it, but because it was fun to have everyone standing round the kitchen stove dipping their bread in the same pot.

'You *have* to do it like that, otherwise it's not dipping day,' said Lisbet.

Then they sealed Christmas presents for an hour or two. They put big red seals on every parcel, with Papa's help. But Lisbet managed to seal her thumb without Papa's help and screamed so that she could be heard all over Junedale.

'There shouldn't be such a thing as sealing wax,' she said when she had finished screaming.

'Of course there should be sealing wax,' said Mardie. 'Otherwise it wouldn't smell of Christmas.'

She explained to Lisbet how nice it would be if you could hide a little of the sealing wax smell in a tin with all the other good Christmas scents. Then you could have the tin to sniff at, all the year round, until Christmas came again at last.

Among Mardie's Christmas presents there was also a parcel for Abe, and in the parcel there was a little mouth-organ. Mardie had bought it with the ghost money she had received after her evening in the Nilssons' wash-house.

Mardie and Abe did not usually give each other Christmas presents, but she was deeply afraid that he was not going to get enough and might be sad about it. So now she had bought him this mouth-organ and just as it was beginning to grow dark she ran across to *Repose*. Lisbet ran after her as fast as she could go.

The Nilssons were in the kitchen as usual and Mr Nilsson was lying on the sofa as usual. But the kitchen was shining with an unusual light. The new lamp was

130

standing on the table, shining brightly, but Abe's eyes were almost brighter still as he looked at it. He could see nothing but the lamp, he scarcely noticed Mardie and Lisbet. But Mr Nilsson gave them a friendly nod from his sofa.

'Junedale's little Mardie and Junedale's Lisbet, you've come just at the right moment.'

He pointed proudly at the lamp.

'What do you think? What do you think of this magnificent article my son has bought, what light, what home comfort!'

'Yes, it's lovely,' said Mardie.

'And look in the parlour! What do you think of the funny Father Christmases my son has put up on the wall? And the Christmas tree he got just to please his old father, what do you think of that? Abe, Abe, you're a good son.'

Mrs Nilsson was sitting as close as she could to the lamp, drinking coffee. She put the cup down now and patted Abe on the head.

'As if he didn't do it for his Ma too! Yes, you really are a good boy, little Abe.'

Abe was embarrassed at so much praise and turned to Mardie and Lisbet.

'What did you want anyway?'

Mardie held out the parcel which she had been hiding behind her back.

'I just wanted to give you a Christmas present, Abe.'

'Me?' said Abe. 'A Christmas present? What for?'

But Mrs Nilsson clapped her hands together in dismay.

'A Christmas present for Abe! We forgot about it.'

She turned reproachfully to Mr Nilsson on the sofa.

131

'Emil, did you remember Abe's Christmas present, by any chance?'

Mr Nilsson was silent. He stared sourly at Mrs Nilsson for a while, and in the end he said peevishly:

'Of course I'm the house-owner, and the property-owner, too, but it so happens I'm a bit short of cash. Anyhow, there's no Christmas present for Abe. Are you upset about it, Abe?'

Abe did not look in the least upset.

'Huh, we've got the lamp, haven't we?'

'And Mardie's Christmas present too,' Lisbet

reminded him.

'Yes, blow me down, I've got a Christmas present from Mardie, haven't I?' said Abe.

He opened the packet and took out the mouth-organ and Mr Nilsson cried out happily.

'A mouth-organ, well, bless my soul! Now you can play something pretty for your old father, Abe.'

It wasn't an expensive, grand kind of mouth-organ but Abe could still get tunes out of it. He sat down by his lamp and played '*Now it's Christmastime again*', with almost all the right notes and was very pleased with his mouth-organ. He played '*Home, Sweet Home*' as well, but that made Mr Nilsson cry, because it was the most beautiful song he knew.

Mardie and Lisbet returned to Junedale satisfied.

'What a nice time we had,' said Lisbet.

'Yes, we really did,' said Mardie. 'What a grand lamp, I wish we had one like it.'

Then evening came. At last evening came and all the Christmas candles were lighted in Junedale.

'Just so that Father Christmas can find his way here in the dark,' said Lisbet.

But Father Christmas would not be coming before seven, he had rung up himself to say so, Papa told them.

If only he could have joined them in the kitchen then! Alma had laid out on the big table all that Junedale could produce; ham and baked rice pudding and pickled fish and spare ribs and sausage and meat balls and herring salad and even more things. Mardie and Lisbet counted up to twenty different bowls and dishes. They were in such high spirits by now they had difficulty in sitting still. The heat from all the

133

candles made their cheeks pink; they talked and laughed, as frisky as little calves, but they didn't do much eating.

But later, when Papa had lighted the Christmas tree and Mama was sitting at the piano, they calmed down. For now it was time to sing all the Christmas carols, nothing felt more like Christmas than that.

> *'Shine over sea and shore,*
> *star from afar.'*

Mardie was so happy that her heart ached. The Christmas candles seemed to shine more brightly when she sang and she herself seemed nicer. She must tell Lisbet at once how sorry she was for everything, although just at that moment she couldn't remember exactly what.

But now Papa was saying:

'Coats on, quickly, Father Christmas will be arriving at any moment!'

And they were all off in an instant, Mama and Papa and Alma and Mardie and Lisbet.

It was dark now but the snow lay white on the ground and the trees, and the stars stood clear and bright above the roof of Junedale.

Mardie and Lisbet held hands and ran down the little path to the stream. Everywhere was quiet, but somewhere far away they could hear the faint sound of bells, yes, yes, Father Christmas was coming! As they stood on the jetty in the darkness and snow and heard the sound of bells coming closer and closer, they shivered with excitement and pressed close to Mama. Oh, now they could see the gleam of a torch down by the bend in the stream, it flared up and shone across the snow, and now they could see the horses and sleigh, yes, yes, Father Christmas was coming! He was sitting in a sleigh, with his white beard and red cloak, and the horses trotted briskly right up to the jetty.

'Whoa!' said Father Christmas, stopping right in front of Mardie and Lisbet. They stood there, dumb with excitement, not daring to say a word. They just stared at Father Christmas with big, round eyes. They looked at the horse too. It was quite an ugly little horse, just like Conker from Appletree Hill. Fancy there being two horses that yellow and that ugly in the world . . . although of course Conker didn't have a black crest like that on his forehead.

'Are there any good children here?' asked Father Christmas, who sounded very good-natured, rather like Tom from Appletree Hill.

'Any good children here – yes, I'll swear to that,' said Papa. 'Mardie and Lisbet are two really good little sweethearts!'

'I see. Well, in that case,' said Father Christmas, heaving a big sack out of the sleigh, in that case, Happy Christmas!' he said. It almost sounded as if he were a little shy.

'Happy Christmas!' cried Mardie and Lisbet and Mama and Papa and Alma.

'Happy Christmas, as I said,' said Father Christmas. Then he whipped up his ugly horse, turned the sleigh and drove back the way he had come, towards Appletree Hill.

They stayed on the jetty as long as they could hear the bells. Then Papa and Alma picked up the sack between them and carried it up to Junedale.

135

Christmas Eve is a long day but it does come to an end at last. The candles burned down, everyone had had their presents, everyone had cracked their nuts, everyone had eaten apples and toffee, no one could manage to dance round the Christmas tree any more. Mardie suddenly put her hands to her face and burst into heart-broken sobs.

'Oh Mama, it's over now, just think, it's over already!'

But when she was in bed with her Christmas presents beside her she was already glad that there would be a new day, when she would read her Christmas books and try out her Christmas skis and play with her Christmas doll which had a sailor suit and was called Katya.

Lisbet also had a doll, a sailor doll which she had christened Abe, and she had Abe in bed with her.

'You certainly are a good boy, little Abe,' said Lisbet, patting him on the head. She lay thinking in silence for some time and then said slowly:

'Of course I'm the house-owner and the property-owner as well, so there's no Christmas present for Abe. But next year,' said Lisbet, patting Abe on the head again, 'next year you'll defuntly get a whole sackful. If I've got any cash, that is!'

136

9
Joseph in the well

Winter would soon be over, and Spring was on its way. Mardie and Lisbet helped the time to go a little faster. The ground was already bare where the sun shone brightest, but on the north side there were still some snow-drifts left. Mardie and Lisbet didn't like them at all. They went for them with their spades and melted the snow in the water barrels by the kitchen door, and suddenly it really was Spring. The small, downy buds of wood anemones were coming out everywhere under

the birches and Mardie and Lisbet knelt to look at them every day to make sure they were growing properly. Starlings had settled in the bird-boxes which Papa had put up round Junedale. Every morning Mardie and Lisbet woke to bird-song. The water was running so high in the stream that it was washing over the jetty. Mardie and Lisbet were not allowed to go down there at all. Instead they played hop-scotch on the garden paths and bounced a ball against the woodshed wall.

But Mardie could not spend all her time playing hop-scotch and throwing a ball, she had a lot of homework now and had to read and write and do sums in the afternoon, sometimes for a whole hour. Mardie thought that was much too long to waste on homework. She could read to herself perfectly, but writing was not so good, and doing sums was worst of all. Sometimes Mardie went to Alma in the kitchen to do her homework. Then Lisbet would sit down in the log corner pretending to be Alma skinning fish. She scraped the logs with a kitchen knife until the bark flew, muttering quietly over the hard-skinned fish, just as she had heard Alma do.

'Blow the fish! If I was the mistress, you wouldn't catch me buying them!'

Lisbet was enjoying herself and she was sorry for Mardie, sitting there labouring over her homework. Sums must be difficult. Sometimes Papa gave Mardie some practice in mental arithmetic so that she could get really good at it. Lisbet also wanted Mardie to do well and she thought out the most complicated sums for her, just as Papa did.

'Mardie,' said Lisbet from her place in the wood

corner, 'if there are ten boys and one has an operation, how many will be left?'

Mardie was not in the least bit grateful for her help and snorted at Lisbet's example.

'Do be quiet! Can't you see I'm doing my Tables!'

But Alma laughed. She thought it was nice of Lisbet to try to teach Mardie mental arithmetic. Alma produced some examples herself.

'If I lay seventeen eggs here on the sofa and take away five . . .' she began, but Mardie shrieked with laughter.

'Ha ha, can you lay eggs, Alma? They why do we buy them from Appletree Hill?'

Lisbet also laughed heartily.

'Ha ha, Alma can lay eggs, so we don't have to buy any from Appletree Hill, I'm going to tell Mama!'

They teased Alma for a long time, and asked her to lay a great many eggs as it would soon be Easter.

Alma didn't give Mardie any more arithmetic problems. She heard her Bible-learning instead. Mardie was good at that. Ida had told her so many of the Bible stories and Mardie was praised at school for knowing as much as she did. But Ida didn't seem to have told her everything.

One day, just before Easter Mardie came home all tear-stained and threw herself on her mother's neck.

'Mama,' she sobbed, 'if you only knew how beastly they were to Joseph!'

It was some time before Mama realised that she meant Joseph in the Bible story; Mardie was sobbing so hard she could scarcely speak. How could there be people as wicked as Joseph's brothers, how could they throw their own brother down a well and sell him as a

139

slave and then go home and tell his poor papa that Joseph had been eaten by a wild beast!

'Yes, but Joseph did very well after that,' Mama tried to comfort her. 'And he did see his papa again, you know.'

Mardie did know, but it didn't help. She sorrowed over Joseph all day long, and it was not until bedtime that she had calmed down enough to tell Lisbet about him.

'Think of that, Lisbet . . . think of selling your own brother as a slave!'

'What's a slave?' asked Lisbet.

'A slave is someone who just works and works and works,' said Mardie.

'Is Papa a slave?' asked Lisbet.

'Pooh, of course he isn't!'

'Yes he is, because he just works and works and works,' said Lisbet.

'Oh, you don't know anything,' said Mardie. 'They beat a slave with a whip. The moment he doesn't want to work, they just beat him.'

'I could borrow a whip from Appletree Hill and beat Papa just a *little*. Then he'd be a slave,' said Lisbet, who thought slaves sounded exciting. Then she went to sleep.

Mardie lay awake for a long time, thinking about Joseph who was sold as a slave by his brothers.

Then it was Easter. The daffodils and narcissus and crocus were blooming round Junedale; the birches had small green leaves, Mardie had Easter holidays and Marie from Appletree Hill came to Junedale with five dozen eggs – since Alma stubbornly refused to lay any. Easter was almost as much fun as Christmas,

Mardie and Lisbet thought. It was fun to eat eggs which were red and blue and green instead of white. Mardie and Lisbet and Papa helped to dye them. And it was fun to have Easter cards. Grandma and their cousins sent such grand ones, with downy chicks and beautiful daffodils on them. But of course the best thing of all was the Easter hare, which came at night when everyone was asleep and put small marzipan eggs in the grass outside the nursery window. This year he had thought of something else to do. He had left two parcels under the laburnum bush. 'For Mardie,' was written on one parcel and 'For Lisbet' on the other. Both parcels contained a little chocolate boy, a doll made of chocolate, in fact Mardie and Lisbet had never seen anything more wonderful.

Mardie christened her chocolate boy Jerry and Lisbet christened hers Berry. All through Easter they played with Jerry and Berry without so much as licking them.

'I shall save Jerry up for as long as I live,' said Mardie. 'I shall never, never eat him.'

'I shall save Berry too,' said Lisbet. 'For as long as I can.'

On the afternoon of the following day Lisbet was alone in the nursery. Mardie was in the kitchen, playing Fox-and-Geese with Alma. As they were sitting there, in came Lisbet with chocolate all over her face.

'I've just eaten Berry,' she said calmly.

Mardie gave a shriek.

'How *could* you? You've eaten your own child!'

Lisbet nodded.

'Yes, that's right. Just like the sow at Appletree

141

Hill, she ate her children, do you remember? There were nine of them, too!'

Mardie thought Lisbet was dreadful.

'You're not the sow at Appletree Hill. You shouldn't behave like a pig.'

'No, so one would think,' said Lisbet, as Alma used to say. 'But it's done now,' she said, nodding happily. She was obviously not the least bit sorry.

But next morning, when Mardie was sitting up in bed playing with Jerry, Lisbet began to be sorry. Perhaps not so much because Berry had gone as that Jerry was still there.

'I tell you what, Mardie,' said Lisbet craftily, 'you eat Jerry up!'

Mardie shook her head.

'Never, never! Not ever!'

She put Jerry to bed in his cigar box. He had cotton wool to lie on and a piece of blue silk as a cover. There was no end to the fun Mardie had with her Jerry. Lisbet was getting more and more sorry and in the end she put her head on one side and pleaded:

'Couldn't I borrow Jerry a bit? I could borrow him *once* anyway, couldn't I?'

'No, you couldn't,' said Mardie.

'How many times?' asked Lisbet.

'Not once, sucks to you,' said Mardie. 'You needn't have eaten Berry up!'

She tucked Jerry into his bed and put the silk coverlet over him and put the bed in the dolls' house.

Soon the Easter holidays were over. Mardie went back to school and Lisbet had to spend all her mornings alone in the nursery.

One day Mardie came home, and what did she find

under the silk coverlet in the cigar box in the dolls' house? No Jerry! Just a poor, wretched little chocolate body without a head. There was a shriek of rage which shook Junedale and Mama came running in a fright, thinking that Mardie was dying, at the very least. But Mardie was lying full length on her bed, roaring:

'Lisbet has bitten Jerry's head off! O-o-o-o-oh!'

Lisbet was out in the garden with Sasso. She was called in and Mama questioned her sternly.

'Did you bite Jerry's head off?'

Lisbet looked to the right and she looked to the left, then she looked straight ahead and said:

'Perhaps I did. But I've forgotten.'

Then Mardie cried louder than ever and Mama scolded Lisbet for a long time. Then she said:

'Now tell Mardie you're sorry, Lisbet.'

Lisbet stood there in dead silence, not moving an eyelash.

'Well?' said Mama.

'Well what?' said Lisbet.

'You must tell Mardie you're sorry.'

'I defuntly won't,' said Lisbet, closing her lips in the stubborn way she had when she was being contrary.

Mama tried to make her understand how naughty she had been and Lisbet certainly understood perfectly, but she would not say she was sorry. Anyway, Mardie thought, Jerry still wouldn't have a head.

Mardie went on crying for some time, before sorrowfully eating what was left of Jerry. Lisbet stood beside her, nagging, for she had absolutely no shame.

'Couldn't I taste just a little bit?'

'Naughty girl,' said Mardie, but she wasn't mean. Lisbet got one of Jerry's legs and then they went out to play together.

'Shall we have a look at the bird's nest?' Mardie suggested.

Lisbet agreed. The bird's nest was in an apple tree at the Nilssons'. Abe had shown it to them. Mardie and Lisbet spent some time looking at the pretty pale-blue eggs, but they did not touch anything.

Beside the apple tree was the Nilssons' old well. It was empty and no longer produced any water. Mardie lifted the rotten lid of the well and looked down and at the same moment she had one of her ideas.

'I know what we can do,' she said. 'We can play Joseph in the Well.'

Lisbet clapped her hands.

'Can I be Joseph?'

Mardie thought about it. She had planned to be

144

Joseph herself, but she knew that Lisbet would never manage to be both the slave-trader and Joseph's wicked brothers at once.

'Yes, all right,' said Mardie, running off to fetch a little ladder which was down by the Nilssons' wash-house. She put it in the well for Lisbet to climb down. The well wasn't very deep and Lisbet, far from being frightened was very perky and cheerful.

Mardie pulled the ladder up . . . this was a good game! She sat on the edge of the well looking down at Lisbet, but instead of Lisbet she saw poor Joseph, who was to be sold as a slave and, oh, how sorry she was for him! But now she was all Joseph's wicked brothers, so she said:

'Sucks to you, Joseph, you're going to the first slave-trader who comes along! We're going to sell you and it serves you right.'

Lisbet was throwing herself into the part.

'Ha ha, then Papa will beat you when you get home.'

'That's what you think,' said Mardie. 'We shall tell him that you were eaten by a wild animal, sucks to you.'

She shuddered as she said this, but if you were Joseph's nasty brothers, that's what you were.

Then Lisbet said:

'Didn't Joseph get any food at all when he was sitting in that well?'

'I don't know . . . perhaps,' said Mardie.

Actually that was rather a good idea of Lisbet's. It would be rather fun to sit on the edge of the well, throwing food down to Joseph, so Mardie said:

'Wait here. Lisbet, and I'll run and get you a sandwich.'

Lisbet was forced to wait in any case, whether she wanted to or not. She couldn't get out of the well without the ladder.

Mardie went first to the larder and prepared a sandwich for Lisbet and one for herself. Then she ran up to the nursery, found pencil and paper and printed on the paper in large letters:

BUTERFUL LITEL SLAVE FOR SALE

It was then that she caught sight of the cigar box, so sadly empty, on the table beside her. Mardie remembered what fun it had been when there was a little chocolate boy in it. Now there was no chocolate boy and it was that stupid Lisbet's fault. Suddenly Mardie began to be angry with Lisbet all over again. She hadn't really forgiven her at all, she knew that now. She was still angry when she came back to the well. But Lisbet didn't know that. She thought it was Joseph's nasty brothers who had come and she was quite ready to be cheeky to them.

'Am I supposed to sit here until I'm dead and not get anything to eat?' she said.

This irritated Mardie still more. She was not playing just then and Lisbet was greedier than the sow at Appletree Hill, Mardie thought.

'You can sit there till you've said you're sorry for biting Jerry's head off,' said Mardie.

From the depths of the well Lisbet looked up at Mardie, deeply offended. There she was, being Joseph, who had never bitten the head off any chocolate boy, and along came Mardie, talking rubbish.

'I defuntly will not,' said Lisbet.

'Naughty girl,' said Mardie. She caught sight of the piece of paper she held in her hand . . . 'BUTERFUL LITEL SLAVE FOR SALE'.

'Then I really am going to sell you for a slave,' she said. 'Just like they did with Joseph. Then perhaps you'll say you're sorry?'

'No, I defuntly will not,' said Lisbet, closing her lips tightly.

Mardie was absolutely enraged by her idiotic stubborness.

'You can stay there, then,' she said, throwing the sandwich down to Lisbet. 'Eat now, because when you're a slave you'll *never* get any food, you can be sure of that!'

Lisbet howled despairingly, but she did not say she was sorry. Mardie waited some time to see if she would, but Lisbet was as stubborn as a mule. She cried, but she did not give in. So Mardie fixed the scrap of paper on the end of a little stick and stuck the stick into the grass beside the well. There it stood, with its awful words: 'BUTERFUL LITEL SLAVE FOR SALE'. Any slave-trader who happened to be passing that way could not fail to see it.

'Serves you right,' said Mardie, going away so that she would not hear Lisbet's despairing screams.

Eating her sandwich, she strolled down to the stream. The water had gone down now and her fishing-rod was lying on the jetty. She baited it with a scrap of liver sausage and sat down to fish. Masses of little minnows were swimming round in the water but they didn't seem to like liver sausage, at least none of them took it. All the same, it was very exciting and Mardie forgot all about Lisbet. When she remembered her at last, she was suddenly remorseful. All her anger had gone. She dropped the fishing-rod and raced back to the well as fast as she could. Long before she got there she was calling:

'Lisbet, I'm coming! Don't worry!'

There was no answer. It was strangely silent, no cries, no screams – *and no Lisbet*! She had gone. The well was empty. But the notice was still there on its stick.

'BUTERFUL LITEL SLAVE FOR SALE' it said, but there was something else as well, printed in ink:

```
I BORT THIS SLAVE
FOR 5p. ISIDOR
TURKISH DOG AND SLAVE-TRADER
```

Poor Mardie! Why couldn't she sink into the ground and never come up again? What had she done . . . dear God, don't let it be true . . . she had sold her own sister as a slave! There was a five pence piece, sure enough, on the side of the well, oh, she was worse than Joseph's brothers, for at least they had been properly paid. Five pence, that was all she had to pay for five wretched little toffees or five humbugs, but she had sold the whole of Lisbet, for a miserable five pence! Mardie was desperate . . . oh, what had she done, oh, poor Lisbet! She had only meant to scare her a little. Who would have thought that a slave-trader would come along right away . . . but those villains could smell out a little slave for sale from a long way off!

Mardie sat quite still on the edge of the well, wailing miserably. Dreadful visions passed before her. Poor little Lisbet; there was the slave-trader, coming to make her work, but of course Lisbet said 'I defuntly will not,' and the whip cracked out. Oh, poor Lisbet, oh, poor seller of Lisbet, poor Mardie! And poor Mama and Papa, now they had lost both their little

girls at once, because Mardie certainly could not go home and tell them she had sold Lisbet to a Turkish dog and slave-trader for five pence, never in all the world! She would rather go off into the forest and live as an outlaw, like Robin Hood.

That disgusting five pence piece was lying on the side of the well. Mardie picked it up with a scream and threw it into the well. Then she rushed out of the gate, crying loudly. She must escape to the forest now, before they found out at home about the awful thing that had happened. But there was something stopping her, she didn't *want* to go to the forest. It would be night soon and how could she bear to be alone then? Wasn't there any other place in the world for someone who had sold her sister as a slave . . . at Ida's, perhaps? Ida was so kind, surely she could hide Mardie in her house and let her lie on the floor like a dog and eat crusts . . . anything at all, if only Mardie didn't have

to live in the woods as an outlaw! Yes, Ida was her
only hope.

Ida jumped when Mardie rushed in through her
front door, choking with sobs.

'I tell you, I tell you, you came running in as if the
police were after you,' said Ida. 'What's the matter
now?'

Mardie stared wildly at her. The police, Ida had
said, yes, there must be a punishment for selling slaves,
the police would have to come and arrest her when
they knew what she had done! With a sobbing cry

Mardie cast herself full-length on the floor in front of Ida and flung her arms round Ida's legs.

'Dear, dear Ida,' she sobbed, 'couldn't I stay on the floor here and just eat crusts?'

'Eat crusts . . . why, for Heaven's sake?' said Ida in astonishment. 'Child, what is the matter? Has something bad happened at Junedale?'

Something bad at Junedale! Mardie burst into heart-broken sobs. Oh, if Ida only knew, then she would realise that things could never by anything but bad at Junedale any more!

'Would you like to tell me about it?' said Ida.

Mardie was so utterly ashamed of her slave-trading that she could not bear to tell Ida about it, but after a great deal of persuasion Ida managed to get out of her that it was something terrible, something so horrible that Mardie could never go home to Junedale again. Ida shook her head sadly.

'I tell you, I tell you, whatever you've done you won't have to lie on the floor and eat crusts.'

Ida picked Mardie up and put her on her bed and tucked a rug round her.

'Have a little sleep,' said Ida. 'It's a great help.'

And almost before she had spoken Mardie was asleep. Slave-trading makes you very tired. There she lay, her face streaked with tears, the lashes dark on her cheeks.

'Poor little soul,' murmured Ida. 'Just you sleep, and I'll be taking myself down to Junedale.'

Mardie slept for a very short time and woke up again with a start. At first she did not know where she was, until she saw the pictures of the brandy flood and the erupting volcano on the wall above the bed. Then she knew, and she also remembered why she was there. Oh, why did she have to wake up again? And where was Ida? Mardie had a terrible thought – what if Ida had gone to fetch the police? There might be a punishment for hiding criminals. Of course Ida was kind, but she wouldn't want to go to prison for Mardie's sake, no, she must have gone for the police.

And now they were coming to fetch her . . . Mardie heard footsteps out in the hall and she could hear Ida talking to someone.

'Go straight in,' said Ida.

With tear-stained eyes Mardie stared at the door. Help, Mama, help! Mama . . . oh, she could never expect any more help from Mama, nor from Papa either, because she had sold their Lisbet as a slave and the police could come and get her whenever they liked and they were coming now . . . now!

The door opened, someone was coming in, someone was standing in the doorway. Not a tall policemen, but

a very small person. Lisbet! Mardie stared as if she had seen a ghost. Oh, Lisbet, could it be true? With a sob Mardie put out her arms, she wanted to feel Lisbet, hold on to her, be sure that it really was her. She wanted to hug her, oh, how much she loved her!

Full of longing and remorse and love, Mardie put out her arms and Lisbet dashed straight into them, but when she got there she gave Mardie a hearty shove,

'Move over, I want to look at the brandy flood too, you've had a look already!'

Lisbet clambered onto the bed and knelt to look at the brandy flood and the volcano, but Mardie could only look at Lisbet, only, only at Lisbet.

'Did you escape from the slave-trader?' she asked shyly, and also with admiration – imagine having such a brave, daring sister!

'What slave-trader?' asked Lisbet. 'Oh, we're not playing that any more. Abe gave me some sugar buns, sucks to you, you didn't get any.'

Mardie stared at her.

'Abe! Was it Abe who got you out of the well?'

Lisbet was staring fixedly at the brandy flood and scarcely heard what Mardie was saying.

'These are the best pictures I've ever seen in my life,' she said.

'*Was* it Abe?' Mardie repeated.

'Yes, of course it was, and I got sugar buns, too . . . Do you know what, Mardie? If I got into the brandy flood I would swim ashore with five strokes, because I can do five strokes, you know!'

'Yes, I know,' said Mardie. 'You're a clever girl, Lisbet, but Abe's a beast!'

Now it was night at Junedale, now the red house by the stream was asleep. The sun had gone down, dusk had fallen among the birches, a blue-dusk, for it was Spring. It was now that the narcissus shone their whitest and smelled their sweetest, it was now that the birches looked their loveliest in their thin green veils under the Spring sky, so cool and clear. And it was quiet. The air had been full of bird-song, but now all the little birds were asleep in their nests and holes.

It was not altogether silent, though. Inside the red house someone was singing:

'Abide with me,
fast falls the eventide,'

they sang. If you stood under the nursery window you could hear it, and someone actually was there, listening. A lanky boy with a shock of fair hair which seemed to light up the darkness. Hidden behind the laburnum bush he stood listening quietly as he had done so often before . . . Abe loved singing. No one knew he was there, and soon he would walk silently away, treading very carefully, for he had no wish to crush the narcissus. The Nobel Lord Abe, Turkish dog and slave-trader, was a very nice boy.

'Abide with me,
fast falls the eventide,'

Lisbet went on singing, although Mama and Papa had already said goodnight and shut the nursery door. But she stopped suddenly.

'Mardie,' said Lisbet, 'can I come into your bed?'

155

'Yes, you can,' said Mardie.

Lisbet trotted quickly across the floor on cold little feet to Mardie's bed.

'Can I lie on your arm?' asked Lisbet.

'Yes, you can, of course you can!'

Oh, how lovely everything was, thought Mardie. She was happy, happy, happy because Lisbet was lying there and was her sister and in Junedale, not in the power of some wicked slave-trader.

Mardie put her arm tightly round Lisbet.

'Lisbet, you must never, never leave me!'

'No, I'm not going anywhere,' Lisbet assured her. 'The main thing is for you and me to be together *always*.'

Outside, the Spring sky was growing darker and darker. It was dark in all the corners of the nursery too, but it was a friendly darkness, Mardie thought. It was their own friendly darkness, hers and Lisbet's, and it felt lovely.

'Mardie,' said Lisbet, pushing her cold little feet in under Mardie's legs. 'Tell me about ghosts and murderers and war!'